"IT'LL INVOLVE A LOT OF TEAMWORK AND COOPERATION."

"Stevie Lake," Max said, his blue eyes twinkling. "I've got something special for you. In honor of the, uh, let's call it friendship, you and Veronica have struck up this morning, I'd like you two to train your horses to pull the Pine Hollow wagon. Girls, you'll have two weeks to turn those saddle horses into a team and give a demonstration for the Cross County Pony Club!"

Stevie couldn't believe her ears. Did Max actually believe that she and Veronica were *friends*? Were they going to have to train their horses together? For a demonstration that *Phil* was going to be watching? She shook her head. Maybe she'd misunderstood. She raised her hand again.

"Max, did I hear you correctly?"

Max grinned and nodded. Carole and Lisa glanced at each other as Stevie buried her face in her hands with a groan. Both of them knew that turning Belle and Danny into a smooth working team was going to be a lot easier than turning Stevie and Veronica into one!

the SADDLE CLUB

DRIVING TEAM

BONNIE BRYANT

A SKYLARK BOOK
NEW YORK · TORONTO · LONDON · SYDNEY · AUCKLAND

Special thanks to Sir "B" Farms
and Laura and Vinny Marino

RL 5, ages 009–012

DRIVING TEAM
A Bantam Skylark Book / January 2000

ISBN 0-553-48677-2

Published simultaneously in the United States and Canada

Bantam Skylark is an imprint of Random House Children's Books, a division
of Random House, Inc. Skylark Books, Bantam Books, and the rooster
colophon are registered trademarks of Random House, Inc. Bantam Books,
1540 Broadway, New York, New York 10036.

PRINTED IN THE UNITED STATES OF AMERICA
OPM   0 9 8 7 6 5 4 3 2 1

*I would like to express my special thanks
to Sallie Bissell for her
help in the writing of this book.*

"Yikes!" Stevie Lake cried as she slipped and fell to one knee in a wide puddle just in front of the stable. Globs of cold, thick mud splattered all over her jeans and shirt. "It's really slick out here!"

"Come on, Stevie!" Carole Hanson motioned to her friend. "Horse Wise is about to begin!"

Stevie sloshed inside the stable, shivering as she pulled her wet sweatshirt close around her neck. The smell of damp hay tickled the inside of her nose as she fought back a sneeze. "I'm glad we're meeting in Max's office," she said. "This weather is really lousy."

"Can you imagine anybody trying to ride in rain like this?" asked Lisa Atwood, who was also waiting for Stevie. She looked up at the driving sheets of water that fell from the gloomy November sky. "You'd probably catch pneumonia, and who knows what your poor horse would catch?"

"Rhinopneumonitis, probably," decided Carole.

"Huh?" Stevie said, frowning.

"I think that's one of Carole's fancy words for a horse cold," laughed Lisa.

Stevie groaned. "I know a fancy word for being late, which is what we're going to be if we don't hurry."

"Then let's go," said Lisa. "We were late for the last meeting. I don't want to get the cold shoulder from Max again."

The three girls hustled through the Pine Hollow stables. It was the place where they had first met and where they had discovered that each was just as crazy about horses as the others. That was when they'd formed The Saddle Club, a club that had only two rules—that the members had to be crazy about horses, and that they had to help each other out whenever possible. Lisa Atwood was the newest to riding, but she was also the oldest and most logical of the trio. Carole Hanson could be scatterbrained about everything from returning her library books to whether her socks matched, but when it came to horses, she was almost an expert and never forgot anything. Stevie Lake, the third member of the club, was often knee-deep in some crazy predicament or practical joke. Though Stevie was as devoted to horses as Carole and Lisa, much of The Saddle Club's time was devoted to getting out of the trouble Stevie's schemes had gotten them into. Still, they had such terrific adventures getting either into or out of their dilemmas that nobody minded.

The girls hurried around a corner, where warm yellow light poured from the open door of Max's office. Maximilian Regnery III was the owner of Pine Hollow, the stables that had been founded by his grandfather Maximilian Regnery I and passed along to him by his own father, Max II. Max now stood behind his desk, chatting with the crowd of young riders who were seated on the floor of his office.

"Well, if it isn't Carole, Lisa, and Stevie." Max checked his watch and grinned. "You're a whole thirty seconds early."

"Hi, Max," Lisa replied as other riders scooted over to make room for them on the floor. "We would have been here sooner, but Stevie had a slight run-in."

Max frowned. "With a horse?"

"Actually, with a mud puddle." Laughing, Stevie held her mud-splashed jeans away from her legs.

Just then Mrs. Reg, who was the stable manager as well as Max's mother, stuck her head into the office.

"Max, have you got a minute to meet a new rider?" she asked.

"Just thirty seconds," he answered.

3

"That's enough."

"I'll be right back," Max said to the assembled Pony Clubbers as he stepped into the hallway.

"Maybe then we can finally begin," said a sarcastic voice from the leather armchair in the corner. "Some of us have been waiting for hours."

The girls turned. The voice belonged to the richest, snootiest girl at Pine Hollow, Veronica diAngelo. She'd curled herself up like a cat in Max's one good chair, wearing a gorgeous green cashmere tunic and sparkling white jodhpurs. The sweater matched her eyes exactly, and it looked expensive. All Veronica's friends sat around the chair, casting admiring glances at her sleek new haircut and beautiful outfit.

"I may be late, Veronica, but at least I came dressed to work," Stevie snapped, her wet sweatshirt still clinging to the back of her neck. "Unlike some people who have the nerve to think that if they come dressed in fancy clothes they can get somebody else to do their chores for them."

"Are you implying that I haven't done any work today?" Veronica's eyes flashed.

Stevie looked at her outfit and shrugged. "I don't know many people who come to muck out stalls dressed in cashmere sweaters."

"I'll have you know that I came early today, mucked out Danny's stall all by myself, and then changed into

4

these clean clothes," Veronica said as her friends Betsy Cavanaugh and Meg Durham nodded in agreement.

Veronica eyed Stevie's tattered sweatshirt and soggy jeans. "In case you haven't noticed, some of us don't like to lounge around in dirty, wet clothes. We prefer to get our work done and leave the muck and dirty straw on the manure pile, instead of bringing cute little samples of it to Horse Wise meetings."

Everyone in the room chuckled. Stevie looked down at her clothes and felt a flush of embarrassment. Mud was caked on both legs of her jeans, and several wisps of hay dangled from the sleeves of her sweatshirt. She looked back at Veronica's spotless outfit and shook her head.

"Sorry, Veronica. But I'm still not convinced you got here early just to get a stall mucked out. I think you must be playing a very late April Fools' trick."

"You don't believe me?" Veronica held out her hands, displaying ten perfectly shaped nails, all painted a delicate pink. "Then come look at the dreadful damage it did to the manicure I got just yesterday!"

Normally Stevie would have ignored Veronica's boasting, but the manicure display was simply too much. She picked her way between Joe Novick and Adam Levine until she stood directly in front of Veronica's chair.

"See?" Veronica held up her nails for inspection.

Stevie bent over and studied them. Though each was still a mostly perfect pink oval, two nails on Veronica's right hand had been recently chipped. Then Stevie took a deep breath and almost passed out from shock. Wafting up from Veronica's delicate white hands was the pungent aroma of horse manure. Veronica was telling the truth. For once in her life, she had actually gotten up early and done some work!

Stevie stood up straight and grabbed one of Veronica's hands, lifting it so that everyone in the room could see. "I want everyone here to know that on this day, Veronica diAngelo actually cleaned out her own horse's stall. She chipped two of her very own fingernails, and her hands have the distinct aroma of *eau de cheval*." She dropped Veronica's hand and turned back toward her.

"I'm sorry for ever doubting you, Veronica," she said with a deep bow. "I had no idea you had become such a hard worker. I apologize for accusing you of being a slacker, and if, in the future, I ever see any little potty accident that some horse might have had on the floor, you'll be the first person I call to clean it up."

With that, the room was filled with snickers. Veronica flopped back in the chair to pout, her own cheeks now pink with embarrassment.

Max returned to the room and tapped a pencil on his desk. "Okay, okay, you guys, let's get this meeting under way. We've got a lot to talk about. Stevie, take a seat. You and Veronica can finish your conversation later."

Stevie crept back to Lisa and Carole and plopped down on the floor just as another deluge of rain beat down on the roof of the barn. Max glanced up at the ceiling, then turned to the assembled riders and grinned.

"I don't know if any of you are aware of this, but in two weeks we're going to have a joint meeting with the Cross County Pony Club."

A murmur of anticipation rippled through the riders. Lisa and Carole grinned at Stevie, whose boyfriend, Phil Marsten, was a member of Cross County. Even though they were equally good riders, there was nothing either of them liked better than competing in some aspect of horsemanship. Their competition was friendly, but Stevie was always looking for an opportunity to show off what she considered her superior riding skills. Phil seemed to have similar notions about his own skills.

"And so"—Max frowned briefly at The Saddle Club girls and cleared his throat—"in honor of all this driving rain that's pelting our barn today, we're going to do projects on driving horses. That'll be the program we present for our meeting with the Cross County club."

"You mean driving horses to shows and trail rides?"

May Grover asked from her spot beside the filing cabinet.

"No," Max explained. "I mean driving horses themselves. Horses pulling wagons and chariots and sulkies."

"Sulkies?" Brittany Lynn piped up. "What's a sulky?"

"That's what Veronica is most of the time," whispered Stevie. Lisa and Carole tried to squelch their giggles.

"Well, that's what I'm hoping we'll find out," said Max. "Driving is a horse sport all by itself—very different from jumping or dressage." Max looked at the riders crowded into his office. "Have I got any volunteers to make reports at the joint meeting?"

Stevie's hand shot up first. There was no way she was going to let an opportunity like this pass by. Max might let her do some special, wonderful report that Phil would remember for the rest of his life! Lisa and Carole raised their hands, too, as did some of the other riders. Soon one of Veronica's manicured hands was waving in the air as well.

"Good." Max beamed. "I'm glad you're excited about this. I think it's going to be a lot of fun. Let's see how I can pair you up, now." He studied the volunteers for a moment and scratched his chin.

"Okay. Lisa Atwood and Carole Hanson, why don't you two work together on a ten-minute report called

'Driving Through History'? That way we can find out what sulkies are."

"Sure, Max," replied Lisa. "Sounds like fun."

"Polly Giacomin and Anna McWhirter, why don't you two give us a ten-minute report on driving tack? There's all sorts of special equipment you need to drive a team of horses."

"Okay." Polly scribbled something in a small notebook and moved over to sit beside Anna.

Stevie's arm grew tired as Max assigned the other reports, until finally only her hand and Veronica's were left waving in the air. It was then that Max looked at her and smiled.

"Stevie Lake," he said, his blue eyes twinkling. "I've got something special for you. In honor of the, uh, let's call it friendship, you and Veronica have struck up this morning, I'd like you two to train your horses to pull the Pine Hollow wagon. Girls, you'll have two weeks to turn those saddle horses into a team and give a demonstration for the Cross County Pony Club!"

Stevie couldn't believe her ears. Did Max actually believe that she and Veronica were *friends*? Were they going to have to train their horses together? For a demonstration that *Phil* was going to be watching? She shook her head. Maybe she'd misunderstood. She raised her hand again.

"Max, did I hear you correctly? You want Veronica and me to turn Danny and Belle into a driving team? And give a demonstration at the joint meeting with Cross County?"

Max grinned and nodded. "You've only got two weeks to get them working together. It'll involve a lot of teamwork and cooperation. Assuming that this rain stops, meet me at the back paddock at four this afternoon, and I'll help you get started."

Carole and Lisa glanced at each other as Stevie buried her face in her hands with a groan. Both of them knew that turning Belle and Danny into a smooth working team was going to be a lot easier than turning Stevie and Veronica into one!

"ANY QUESTIONS?" MAX looked over the group at the end of the meeting. "Okay, then. Let's go tack up. We'll have a flat class in the indoor ring in twenty minutes."

For a moment, as everyone got up and scurried out of the room around her, Stevie just sat on the floor.

"Stevie, are you all right?" Carole leaned over and looked worriedly at her friend.

"I think I must be in shock," Stevie answered. "Can you imagine two whole weeks of working side by side with Veronica?"

Carole shook her head. "Actually, I can't. I don't think I have the patience."

Stevie wrinkled her nose. "And you think I do?"

"I guess Max thinks you have something," Carole said with a shrug.

"I think I have incredibly bad luck," complained Stevie. "And everything could have been so great, too. I mean, I could have done a super report and really impressed Phil. We haven't seen each other in weeks. It would have been nice to show him something that I had put a lot of effort into."

"Stevie, don't you mean *show off* something you'd put a lot of effort into?" Lisa teased gently.

"Well, maybe I do tend to show off a teeny bit in front of Phil," Stevie admitted.

"Oh, this might not be so bad, Stevie," Carole said. "If anybody can pull something fantastic out of the hat with Veronica, it's you."

"Maybe I could just shove Veronica back into the hat," grumbled Stevie. "That would be fantastic enough for me."

"Look," said Carole. "Just don't think about any of this right now. Let's go tack up the horses. We haven't seen them since last Wednesday's class!"

"You're right," said Stevie, hopping to her feet. "I'm losing sight of what counts here. Being with Belle is far more important than worrying about Veronica."

They hurried back down one of the long stable corridors. Carole's gelding, Starlight, was stabled next to

Stevie's mare, Belle, and both horses' heads were poked expectantly out of their stalls.

"Belle!" Stevie cried. "How I've missed you!" She reached up and gave the pretty bay mare a delicious scratch behind the ears.

"Starlight!" Carole echoed Stevie's sentiments as her horse gave a soft nicker. She hugged him gently around the neck, pressing her cheek against his soft brown hair. "Hi, big guy!" she whispered. "I've missed you!"

"I'm going to get Prancer," Lisa called. "I'll cross-tie her up here so we can talk."

"Okay," said Stevie and Carole as they hurried into the tack room to get their saddles and grooming supplies. By the time they got back, Lisa already had Prancer tied just a few feet away.

"Look," she called as Prancer nuzzled Starlight's ear. "I think even the horses have missed being with each other."

"I know they've missed riding," said Carole. "It's too bad we can't go for a trail ride after class."

"I know," said Stevie. "If we did, though, we'd probably all come down with rhino-newmo-whatever-it-is."

"Rhinopneumonitis," corrected Carole. "And you're right. We probably would. Anyway, Lisa and I ought to start thinking about our report on the history of driving."

The girls began to brush their horses. Carole curried

dried mud from Starlight's withers while Lisa picked out Prancer's hooves. Stevie worked in silence, brushing Belle's thick coat of winter hair. The idea of working with Veronica was hard enough to think about; talking about it would only make it worse. She decided to concentrate on Belle and just listen to all the plans her friends were making.

"We could go over to the library and see what kinds of books they have on driving," Lisa was saying. "And we could start from the very first drivers known to man."

"Right," replied Carole. "Like Helios, the Greek god who drove his chariot across the sky every day, pulling the sun with it."

Lisa smoothed a saddle pad on Prancer's back. "Then we could just come down through history: the old Roman chariots and the Russian troikas and the hospital wagons that rescued the wounded soldiers in the Civil War."

"And the twenty-mule-team wagons that helped settle the West." Carole cinched up Starlight's saddle. "And the old coaches that were early versions of buses. And sulkies, and . . ."

Lisa nodded. "There's tons of material out there. We just have to figure out how to cram it all into a ten-minute report."

"Want to stop by the library after class?" Carole asked.

"Sure," said Lisa. "It might take us two weeks just to figure out what we want to say."

Just then they heard a sad sigh from the other side of Belle.

"Stevie?" Carole asked. "Is that you?"

"Yes," Stevie replied glumly. "I'm just listening to what a great time you guys are going to have working on your project while I'll be stuck here with You-Know-Who."

"Oh, Stevie, maybe it won't be so bad." Lisa adjusted the bit in Prancer's mouth. "Maybe she really has changed for the better. Maybe she'll come early in grubby clothes to work on the driving project."

Stevie tightened Belle's girth. "Yeah. And the moon's made of green cheese, and there's a pot of gold at the end of every rainbow."

Lisa shrugged. "I know Veronica's changing might be far-fetched, but it's not absolutely, totally impossible."

Stevie sighed again. "But I don't want to spend ten minutes with that creepy girl, much less two weeks. Plus, I'll actually have to try to cooperate with her!" Stevie shook her head. "The only time I ever have any fun with Veronica is when I insult her!"

Lisa laughed. "Well, I guess the next two weeks are just going to be a real challenge for you."

Carole snapped on her hard hat. "Stevie, Veronica probably messed up her manicure so badly this morning that she'll beg off doing any more work for the next two weeks. You won't have to put up with her at all."

"Right!" cried Lisa. "You'll be free to do the whole project yourself!"

Stevie's honey blond hair seemed to stand on end. "That's the good news? I get to train two saddle horses to drive as a team and put on a demonstration in front of Phil all by myself? In two weeks?"

Carole frowned. "Well, okay, maybe that's not such good news, but look at it this way: It might be the best thing in the world if Veronica doesn't show up. Agreed, she's a rotten human being, but she's got a wonderful horse. Danny's a smart, willing animal, and training him should be a piece of cake. You'll be the star of the whole show, and Phil will be there to see it all!"

Stevie buckled Belle's chin strap, then grinned. "You know, you might be right. It would be hard, training two horses all alone, but if I could pull it off, it would be spectacular!"

"Why don't we just concentrate on having a spectacular flat class now, Stevie?" said Lisa. "Then we can all three think about the Veronica problem afterward."

"Okay," Stevie replied, once again smiling as she led Belle toward the indoor ring.

THE INDOOR RING had been cleared of all jumps and cavalletti, and most of the Horse Wise riders were waiting for class to begin. When Stevie saw that Veronica was at one end of the ring talking to Polly and Betsy, she led Belle to the opposite end. Lisa and Carole followed.

"How come we're going over here?" Lisa asked.

"I don't want to ride too close to Veronica," replied Stevie. "Some of my dirt samples might accidentally rub off on her."

Carole glanced over her shoulder. "At least she's not riding in her cashmere sweater," she giggled.

"That means she's changed clothes three times already this morning, and it's not even ten o'clock." Lisa shook her head. "That must be some kind of record."

Suddenly the girls heard a loud clap. Max strode to the center of the ring. "Okay, everybody. Mount and warm up for about five minutes. Then we're going to do some exercises in pairs."

"What's this thing with pairs Max has today?" Stevie asked as she climbed up on Belle. "Why can't we work as trios?"

17

"Beats me," Carole replied. "Maybe this is Max's Promote Harmony by Riding in Pairs campaign."

"Well, I'm all for that," said Stevie. She glanced at Veronica. "Only some of us need to become distinctly more harmonious."

The girls started walking their horses slowly around the ring, building up to an extended walk and finally a slow trot. It felt good to get their stiff riding muscles limbered up, and by the time Max had clapped his hands again, all the horses and riders were ready for the lesson. Even Stevie felt good. All problems, she decided, looked smaller from the back of a horse.

"Okay." Max walked to the center of the ring. "Today we're going to work on some fairly simple exercises, but we're going to work on them in close pairs, side by side. It's important that you and the person you're teamed up with work together and cue your horses into making these gait changes smoothly and at the same time. Understand?"

When everyone nodded, Max continued. "Okay. Let's choose partners. Everyone who's working with someone on a driving project, just pair up with your partner. Everybody else team up with the rider behind you."

For a moment everyone scrambled to get a partner. Lisa and Carole trotted to the side of the ring, happy to be teamed up, but Stevie gulped as she tried hard to remember what she'd just decided about problems looking smaller from the back of a horse. Veronica diAngelo and Danny were walking straight toward her and Belle.

"Veronica." Stevie sighed. "Looks like we're on the same team again."

Veronica tossed her head and scowled.

When everyone was ready, Max waved his hands for their attention. "Okay, move with your partner to the outside of the ring and start walking clockwise."

Stevie tried to smile. "Do you want to be on the left or right?"

"Oh, please," said Veronica. She turned Danny sharply to the right and began walking behind Polly and Anna. Stevie had to hurry to catch up.

"Do you want the inside or the outside of the ring?" Stevie asked again as she pulled Belle up beside Danny.

"It doesn't matter a bit to Danny," sniffed Veronica as she cast a disdainful glance at Belle. "He's a Thoroughbred. He can do anything."

"Well, so can Belle—" Stevie sputtered, only to be cut short by the sound of Max's voice.

"Okay, riders, go three strides at the walk, then go into an extended trot *together*, *at the same time*. And don't run up on your neighbor's rear end. I don't want anybody kicked today."

Stevie began to count Belle's strides. Just before she

asked Belle for a trot, Veronica and Danny hopped out ahead, already trotting briskly. Stevie squeezed Belle with her legs, trying to catch up. They trotted, out of balance, halfway around the ring.

"Okay," called Max. "That was pretty good. Now I'm going to count. When I say *five*, I want you all to ask for a canter. But remember, ask for it *together*." He looked at Stevie and Veronica. "Some of you guys look like you're riding horses on a merry-go-round. Okay. One, two . . ."

By the time Max reached *three*, Stevie had caught up with Veronica. "Can you give me some kind of signal when you're going to change leads?" Stevie whispered.

"No!" snapped Veronica. "I need to concentrate on Danny. You just watch us and do what we do."

Stevie tried to watch Danny's and Belle's front legs at the same time. Just before Max called out "five," Veronica pushed Danny into a canter. Stevie did the same, trying to stay together, but Veronica had asked Danny for the wrong lead. He and Belle cantered around the ring, almost bumping into each other in the turn. Finally Stevie asked Belle to make a flying lead change just to avoid having the two horses cantering together so awkwardly.

"Okay." Again Max aimed a sharp glance at both of them. "Everybody walk."

Stevie and Veronica pulled both horses down into a walk. "Why can't we work out some kind of signal for what we're going to do?" Stevie whispered. "Max doesn't look too happy with our performance."

"I'm sure Max is perfectly pleased with the way Danny and I are performing." Veronica raised one eyebrow. "You and Belle, on the other hand . . ." She gave Stevie a sickeningly sweet smile. "I'm sure he knows you're doing the best you can."

"But—" Stevie began, feeling her blood pressure rising.

"Okay, everybody," Max called. "Some of you are doing great. Others can stand a little more practice in cooperation. Since you're all facing the same direction, let's all try a half turn to the right."

Stevie pulled Belle up beside Danny, listening to Max's instructions.

"Go into a sitting trot, then everybody circle to the right, then ride a straight line back to where you started. You and your partner should make one big half circle together." Max looked at the riders. "Everybody ready? Then go!"

Stevie urged Belle into a trot, then applied gentle pressure to Belle's right side with her leg. Belle responded perfectly, turning in a circle, but Danny balked midway through the turn. He stopped once; then, instead of walking beside Belle, he lunged ahead of her. Stevie had to grab Belle's mane while the poor horse almost stood on her toes to keep from being run over.

"Okay, okay, everybody stop!" Stevie heard Max call, his voice suddenly disgusted. She looked over her shoulder and saw him coming toward them.

"Stevie and Veronica, these are easy, elementary exercises, and not once have you been together on anything. What's going on with you two?"

"It's not me!" cried Veronica. "Danny and I have executed your instructions perfectly, right on time. Stevie and Belle are slow. They can't keep up!"

Stevie had just opened her mouth to say that Veronica was the one who was constantly jumping the gun and refusing to work out any signals when she saw Max's blue eyes flash. She knew from experience that it was not the time to explain her position with regard to Veronica. Max wasn't interested in excuses, just results. She took a deep breath.

"Sorry, Max," she said softly. "I guess we are having some problems. We'll just have to concentrate harder, I suppose."

"I suppose so," Max said thoughtfully, glancing at Veronica. "Well, let's try it again." He turned and walked back to the middle of the ring. "Okay, everybody, get back to your original positions!"

This time Stevie waited to see which way Veronica was going to go before she moved Belle one inch. *Oh, brother*, she thought as Veronica pulled Danny in an unnecessarily huge circle. *If this is what working with Veronica's like, I've got a long two weeks ahead of me!*

"STEVIE, WHAT ARE you going to do?" Carole and Lisa peeked over the stall door, where Stevie was working a burr from Belle's tail.

Stevie sighed. "I'm just going to hang around here until Max meets with us to explain the driving tack." She held up the prickly burr and examined it. "I wish I were going with you guys, though."

"We wish you were, too," said Carole. "But maybe this won't be as bad as you're expecting. Veronica might actually have turned over a new leaf."

"Right," said Stevie. "If her behavior in the flat class was any indication, she's turned from obnoxious all the way over to unbearable."

"Oh, Stevie, I think she just got mad," said Lisa.

24

"You did make everybody laugh at her at the Horse Wise meeting."

"Well, she got me back. She made me look like a real jerk in front of Max." Stevie smoothed Belle's tail. "You guys may as well go on to the library and have some fun. I'll just wait here and see what Miss Cashmere Sweater's going to do."

"We hate to leave you, but we do need to get to work," said Carole.

"Don't worry about it." Stevie forced herself to smile. "At least I've got Belle to keep me company. She's a lot more fun than Veronica any day. I'll see you later."

Carole and Lisa said good-bye, then turned and hurried to the bus stop at the end of the long Pine Hollow driveway.

"I hate to leave Stevie like this," said Lisa as their boots sloshed through the soggy drive. "I feel like she really needs us right now."

"I do, too," Carole replied. "But what can we do? Max made the assignments. All we could do would be hang around and watch the disaster unfold." She shuddered. "It might be too horrible to watch."

"You're right," said Lisa. "And then we'd be too upset to get our own project done." She sighed and ran her hand through her shoulder-length blond hair. "I guess Stevie's going to have to get through this on her own."

After a short ride across town, the girls got off the bus in front of the big redbrick library, where two stone lions guarded the doors.

"Do you have anything we can take notes on?" Lisa asked, stopping in front of the library door.

"No," said Carole. "I bring more apples and carrots to Pine Hollow than I do paper and pens."

"Then why don't we go into that stationery store across the street and pick up some note cards? We'll probably find a lot of information we'll need to write down."

They hurried across the wet street to the stationery store, where Lisa bought three packs of four-by-six index cards and two pencils. Carole bought a tiny horse bookmark and a pack of butterscotch.

"In case we get hungry," she said as Lisa gave her a quizzical look. "My dad says it's okay to eat candy in the library as long as you don't throw the wrappers on the floor."

"Whatever," laughed Lisa as they splashed back across the street and hurried between the two big lions.

Inside, the library was a cheery, warm hive of activity. Bright lights shone overhead as people checked out books, clicked away at computers, read magazines, and researched projects at the long tables.

"Where shall we start?" whispered Carole.

"Why don't I see what I can find on the library's catalog while you check out the horse section?" suggested Lisa. "Do you know where it is?"

"Six-thirty-six in the Dewey decimal system," reported Carole with a smile. "I've spent about a jillion hours there."

"Then see what you can find, and I'll meet you over there when I finish at the computer."

"Okay."

Carole walked to the corner of the library that held all the animal books, while Lisa found a free computer terminal. She sat down and opened her note cards, then started searching the library's catalog by typing in the word *chariot* in the subject field. She punched Enter, and a few seconds later all the titles concerning chariots flashed on the screen. Lisa wrote them all down, then typed in the word *stagecoach*. An instant later the computer listed seven books about stagecoaches. In just a little while, Lisa had a pile of index cards filled with books about driving.

Research doesn't take long at all when you've got a computer doing the legwork, she thought. *Wish they'd assign us our own computers in school, just like they give us math and English books.*

When she'd researched all the driving topics she could remember, she hurried over to find Carole. At

27

first she didn't see her, but then she turned a corner in the stacks, and there sat her friend with a pile of eighteen books in front of her.

"Gosh," said Lisa, "looks like you're finding a lot. I got a bunch of titles from the computer, too."

Carole frowned at the books she'd gathered. "I bet there are still more. Let's go ask the librarian."

Lisa followed Carole over to the return desk, where a pretty blond woman in a bright blue sweater was putting books on a cart. She smiled as both girls approached the counter.

"Hi, girls," she said sweetly. "I'm Mrs. Davidson. Can I help you find something today?"

"Yes. We need all the books you've got on driving," Carole said.

"Driving?" Mrs. Davidson blinked. "Aren't you a little young to be studying for your licenses?"

"Oh, no," Lisa laughed. "Not car driving. We mean horse driving. Like carriages and wagons and things like that."

"Oh." Mrs. Davidson chuckled. "I see. You mean team driving. Let me see. I believe I shelved a book on team driving just the other day."

She stuck a pencil behind one ear and bustled out from behind the counter. "If I remember, it's right over here." She walked quickly to an area of the stacks Carole had never been in before, reached up to the top shelf, and pulled down a thick red book titled *Customs and Carriages*.

"Great," said Carole, thumbing through the book. "Are there any more?"

"Give me a few minutes," said Mrs. Davidson, "and I'll see what I can find."

Carole and Lisa moved the books Carole had gathered to a table while Mrs. Davidson fluttered from shelf to shelf, adding volumes to their collection.

"Okay," Mrs. Davidson said a few minutes later, when the tabletop was covered with books. "I think that's it."

"Gosh," said Lisa, counting quickly. "That's forty-three books on driving."

"Is that enough?" asked Mrs. Davidson.

"I think so," laughed Carole. "Thank you so much, Mrs. Davidson. We could never have found that many books by ourselves."

"My pleasure," Mrs. Davidson said cheerily as she went back to the return desk. "I never mind helping young readers with a project."

"Wow." Lisa eyed the huge selection of books. "Where should we start?"

Carole frowned. "Why don't we go through these and reshelve the ones that won't be much help— you know, the ones that are too babyish or too technical?"

"Good idea," said Lisa. "I'll sift through the ones at this end of the table. You take the ones down there."

Carole sat down and opened the first book. The title was perfect—*Driving Through History*—but she realized after she'd thumbed through the first few pages that it was a fictional story about a pair of guys in a magical car that travels through time. Carole checked to make sure the guys hadn't driven near any ancient chariots, then rose to her feet. "This one looks interesting, but it's not going to help us with our report. I think I'll reshelve it."

"Okay," said Lisa. "I'll stay here and go through these."

Carole found the empty spot where the book belonged. It was on a shelf just above the floor. She got down on her hands and knees to shove the book into the right slot and found herself peeping through to the other side of the stack. Standing on a stool in the next aisle were a pair of small red sneakers, which were under a small pair of blue jeans, which were apparently attached to a little kid. It seemed to Carole as if the child was trying to hide in the dingiest corner of the library. Quietly she reshelved the book and leaned forward to peek around the stack.

A little girl stood there. She wore a red wool sweater along with her jeans and had curly hair, almost as blond as Mrs. Davidson's. Though she was standing as if she wanted to be invisible, in her arms she clutched one of Carole's all-time favorite books, *Misty of Chincoteague* by Marguerite Henry.

"Hi," said Carole, barely above a whisper. "That's a great book, isn't it?"

The little girl nodded.

"I just adore it. Have you gotten to the race parts yet?"

"I don't know." The little girl shrugged. "I can only look at the pictures."

Carole frowned. "How come?"

"Because I can't read yet."

"Oh," said Carole. "I see." She leaned against the bookshelf with a dreamy look in her soft brown eyes. It had been seven or eight years since she had learned to read, but she could still remember sitting on her mother's lap, running her fingers over the words in her horse books. They had all seemed so wonderful and mysterious, and she'd hardly been able to wait to go to school so that she could learn to read the stories about these great animals whose pictures she loved. Now she couldn't imagine not being able to read, especially about horses.

Carole smiled at the little girl. "How old are you?"

"Five." The little girl held up all the fingers on one hand. "My name's Cynthia and I just started kindergarten."

31

"Hey, that's great," said Carole. "That means you'll be reading in about a year. Then you can check out all these wonderful books about horses and read them all you want."

"But I want to know what happens to the horses in this book now." Cynthia's lower lip stuck out as if she might cry. Carole moved closer and sat down beside her.

"Well, let's see," she said. "Maybe I can explain what's going on."

She thumbed through the book and smiled at the illustrations she remembered so well. "This is the fierce pony stallion the Pied Piper, who's chasing the great mare Phantom back to the herd, away from Paul and Maureen, who want to catch her."

Carole turned the pages, explaining the pictures. "Here Paul and Maureen are working hard to earn enough money to buy the Phantom, if they can catch her on Pony Penning Day. And here Paul has to jump in the water to save Phantom's foal, Misty, from drowning in the sea!"

"Wow," said Cynthia. "How can you tell what's going on just by looking at the pictures? Not even my teacher at kindergarten can do that."

Carole laughed. "Well, this is one of my most favorite books. I bet I've read it about fifty times. I could almost tell you what happens from memory."

"Could you?" asked Cynthia excitedly. "Would you?"

"Sure," answered Carole, settling back against the bookcase. "About five hundred years ago Misty's pony ancestors were shipped from Spain to work in the gold mines of Peru, but a great storm blew in and wrecked their ship. The ponies broke free and finally swam ashore on Assateague Island. . . ."

"Carole?" a familiar voice rang out. "What on earth are you doing?"

Carole looked up. Lisa stood there, pencil and note cards in hand.

"Oh, hi, Lisa." Carole gave a sheepish grin. "I was just reading, uh, *Misty*."

"Reading *Misty*?" Lisa frowned. "I thought you were reshelving books we didn't need."

"Well, I was, but this little girl was trying to figure out *Misty* just by looking at the pictures, and I thought I'd help her out. Her name's Cynthia, and she likes books about horses."

"Hi, Cynthia." Lisa knelt down and smiled. "My name's Lisa. How old are you?"

"Five," Cynthia replied shyly.

"Do you go to school?"

"I go to kindergarten, but my teacher hasn't taught me how to read yet."

Lisa smiled again. "You know there are brighter, nicer places to look at books than this dark old corner of the stacks. Why don't you move to one of the children's tables?"

For a long moment Cynthia stared at the floor. "Because I need to hide," she finally replied, her voice just a whisper.

"Hide?" Lisa looked at Carole and frowned. "How come?"

"Because that mean old Mrs. Davidson would be real mad if she found me here again."

Carole looked at Cynthia. "But why? Mrs. Davidson loves to see kids use the library. She helped us gather lots of books about driving."

Cynthia dug the toe of her right sneaker into the carpet. "Mrs. Davidson has found me here before. She doesn't like it when my mother leaves me here."

"Your mother leaves you here?" Lisa's voice rose in alarm.

Cynthia nodded. "She leaves me here to go to the mall and shop. She buys all sorts of stuff. I bet she spends a million dollars a week at the mall." She gave a loud sniff.

Lisa and Carole exchanged glances. "Just like You-Know-Who," Carole said softly, thinking of Veronica diAngelo and her mother, who seemed to spend half their lives driving from mall to mall looking for stuff to buy.

"So, does your mom leave you here for a long time?" Carole asked.

Cynthia nodded. "She's not going to pick me up today until six."

"*Six?*" Lisa cried. "Cynthia, the library closes at five-thirty. Do you just wait on the steps for her all by yourself?"

Cynthia gave a big sigh and looked at the floor again.

"Carole, this is terrible. We've got to do something. No five-year-old should be left at the library all day while her mother shops at the mall!"

"I know," said Carole. "Let's go tell Mrs. Davidson. She'll know what to do."

"No, please!" cried Cynthia. "Mo—Mrs. Davidson would be so mad! She would call my mother and throw me out and never let me come back again. Then I could never find out what happened to Misty!"

"Okay, okay, calm down." Carole put one arm around the little girl and gave her a hug. "We won't tell Mrs. Davidson."

"No, we won't," added Lisa. "We promise."

"Thanks," said Cynthia, blinking back tears. She held up her book. "Do you think you could read me a little bit more of *Misty* before my mom comes?"

Lisa and Carole looked at each other. "Sure," they

35

said together, settling down on either side of Cynthia. "We'll take turns reading you a chapter apiece."

"Gosh," Cynthia said. "You two are great!"

Carole and Lisa had just started reading about Paul's adventures on Pony Penning Day when the library lights flickered twice. Carole stopped reading and looked at her watch.

"Good grief!" she cried. "It's five-fifteen! The library's going to close in fifteen minutes, and we haven't gotten anything done except pile up a big stack of books."

"We'd better get Mrs. Davidson to put them on reserve for us," said Lisa.

"You won't tell her about me, will you?" Cynthia shrank back in the corner again.

"Oh, no. We're just going to make sure nobody will check out our driving books before we've finished with them," Lisa explained as she and Carole got to their feet. "Will you be okay back here?"

"Yes. I'll just wait till Mrs. Davidson isn't looking, then I'll sneak out the front door. Mostly, she never even knows I've been here."

Carole and Lisa shook their heads. "Well, it's been fun reading to you, Cynthia," Carole said with a smile.

"You've been great." Cynthia grinned. "Thanks a lot!"

"Bye," whispered Lisa as she and Carole picked up

their note cards. "Maybe we'll see you again some-time!"

Cynthia smiled and waved, then scooted back into the dark shadows of the tall bookcases.

"Do you believe that?" Carole asked Lisa. "How could someone leave a neat little kid like that to go shopping for hours at the mall?"

"I don't know," replied Lisa. "But then, I never would have dreamed that Mrs. Davidson could be so nice to us and so mean to little Cynthia."

"I know," said Carole. "I guess it just goes to show that appearances aren't always what they seem."

"You mean you can't judge a book by its cover!" Lisa said with a grin. Carole groaned and began stacking their books.

"BELLE, YOU HAVEN'T looked this good in weeks!" Stevie stepped back in the stall to admire her handiwork. All afternoon she'd groomed Belle while waiting for four o'clock to come, and now the mare sparkled. Her mane and tail were free of tangles, her soft coat glistened with a deep chestnut shine, and each of her hooves had been polished to a horse-show luster. She even seemed pleased with herself. Her dark eyes twinkled and she held her head high, as if she knew her owner had taken extra good care of her that day.

Stevie smiled, then jumped as someone whistled right behind her. She turned around. Max stood there.

"Looks like somebody got a beauty treatment today," he said, taking note of Belle's gleaming hooves. "Even a manicure, I see. You're not starting a nail salon for horses, are you?"

"Hardly," said Stevie. "I was just putting myself to good use until four o'clock."

"Well, you've done a great job. Belle looks like she could enter the National Horse Show right now." Max looked at Stevie, his blue eyes kind. "Are you ready to learn about driving?"

Stevie nodded.

"Then meet me in the back storage room in five minutes."

"Okay." Stevie watched as Max returned to his office; then she dug in her pocket for a carrot for Belle. She held it out, and Belle nibbled the tidbit gently from the palm of her hand. "Thanks, girl," Stevie whispered. "You cleaned up like a dream. Now Max thinks I can do at least one thing right!"

She gave Belle a hug, then hurried out of the stall and down to the back storage room. Max had already turned the lights on, and Stevie could see lots of the props and jumps they'd used for Pony Club rallies and gymkhanas of the past. An old candy-striped jump brought a smile to her lips. That had been the first jump she and Belle had gone over together.

"Okay." Max suddenly appeared in the door. "Has your partner shown up yet?"

Stevie shook her head. "Not yet."

"Well, I'll show you everything and let you get started." He crossed the room and pulled a huge box from behind a cardboard figure of Uncle Sam that they'd used for Fourth of July games. Stevie could see that the box was bulging with different kinds of reins and bridles, and in fact it was so heavy that Max could only drag it across the floor.

"Well, here it is," he said, stopping when the box rested in front of Stevie. "The Pine Hollow Driving Tack Collection."

Stevie looked down at the box in dismay. Reins and bridles were tangled up much like the Lakes' big box of Christmas lights in their attic. Dirt and mud encrusted the leathers, and a thin layer of dust covered everything on the top of the pile.

Stevie looked at Max dubiously. "Guess it's been a while since the wagon's been driven, huh?"

"A while," he admitted. He reached into the box and pulled out a cracked bellyband. "I think the D-level Pony Clubbers must have been doing some kind of project with this tack. They're the only ones who would have left everything in such a mess." He frowned. "I'll have to have a chat with them."

Stevie gave an inward shudder. She'd been the recipient of several of Max's chats, and she knew what the D-level kids were in for. Suddenly, though, she smiled. Maybe those little kids had done her a big favor with-

40

out even knowing it. Maybe the tack was in such bad shape that Max would assign her some other project that didn't include working with Veronica diAngelo. Softly she cleared her throat as she peered down into the box.

"So I guess this stuff is in too bad a shape to use, huh?"

"Oh, no," said Max cheerily. "With a little saddle soap and elbow grease, it'll be good as new." He turned to her and grinned. "Just follow me."

With a sigh Stevie followed him as he dragged the box to a relatively empty hallway and turned on the lights overhead.

"This is what driving tack is supposed to look like." Max pulled a pen from his shirt pocket and drew a diagram on the side of the box. "These are the reins, those are the cruppers, here's the checkrein and back pad. All that should be in this box. Why don't you follow this drawing and see if you can lay it out on the floor here? After that, you and Veronica can clean it all up."

Stevie compared the straight lines of the diagram to the tangled mess in the box and frowned. "You want me to make that out of this?"

"That's right." Max rose to his feet. "It shouldn't even take you that long. I'll check back with you in a little while to see how you're doing." He gave her a quick wink, then turned and walked back to his office, leaving her alone in the empty hallway.

"Okay," Stevie said softly, blinking at the dusty box. "Whatever you say."

For what seemed like hours, she worked at detangling reins from bridles, and traces from breechings. When she had finally laid out something that resembled Max's drawing, she heard footsteps echoing down the hall.

"Stevie!" Max called out. "Help has arrived!"

Stevie looked up, hoping that Max had gotten Red O'Malley, the head stable hand, to rescue her from this huge tangle of tack. Instead, her heart sank. Not Red O'Malley but Veronica diAngelo walked beside Max, once again clad in emerald green cashmere. Apparently she was going to work on this project after all.

"Here's your partner," Max said. "You can fill her in on what I told you." Again he turned and walked back to his office. Veronica stood there looking at the harness stretched out on the floor, her nose wrinkling in disgust.

"What on earth are you doing?" she asked.

"I'm turning this jumbled-up box of tack into a driving harness," said Stevie. "And you're supposed to be helping."

"Oh, I had lunch at the country club with my parents." Veronica giggled. "We met some friends from

France, and it went on a lot longer than I expected. You know how the French are about their *déjeuners*."

Stevie glared at her. "No, but I do know how Max is about his Horse Wise assignments. Why don't you grab the end of that trace and help me work on this tack?"

"You actually want me to touch that stuff?" Veronica blinked at Stevie. "I'll get this outfit all grimy with dried horse crud!" She shook her head. "I think Max must have had something else in mind for me."

Stevie looked down at the box. Suddenly she had an idea. An impish little smile flashed across her face, and she turned her gaze back to Veronica.

"You know, Veronica, I think you're absolutely right! Max would never dream of asking anybody who came to the stable in cashmere to do anything that might get them dirty. Why don't you go tell him you need something cleaner to do?"

Veronica lifted one eyebrow. "Do you think he'd listen?"

"I can almost guarantee it," Stevie replied, trying to make her voice sound sincere.

"Well, for once you've had a good idea, Stevie Lake!" Veronica turned and hurried back down the hall to Max's office.

For a moment Stevie was tempted to tiptoe down the hall and listen at the door. She was dying to hear Max's reply to the gullible Veronica, but she knew if he

43

caught her eavesdropping, she'd be in as much trouble as Veronica. "No," she finally told herself. "Just concentrate on this tack and see what happens."

She concentrated on uncoiling the other trace in the box and laying it out beside the first one. Soon she heard footsteps coming down the hall. She looked up. Veronica trudged toward her, now wearing her oldest, dirtiest sweatshirt and a pair of tattered riding breeches.

"Gosh, Veronica, what happened?" Stevie cooed. "Didn't Max have a clean job for you?"

"No!" Veronica's face was bright red. "He told me I needed to reevaluate my attitude toward barn work. Then he told me to come back here and ask you what you wanted me to do." She looked at Stevie. "Well, what do you want me to do?"

"Get busy and sort out this tack," said Stevie. "This is what we're going to use in our demonstration."

Veronica sighed again and flopped down on the floor. She poked around in the box for a moment, then pulled out an odd-shaped piece of leather that was studded with brass buttons.

"Ugh," she said, holding up the dirty piece of tack as if it were a strange object from outer space. "What in the world is this thing?"

"I don't know yet," said Stevie. "This is kind of like a big puzzle. Why don't you saddle soap it and put it

44

over in the mystery pile? Then we can piece everything together later."

"Oh, whatever," groaned Veronica. She got up and walked to the tack room, returning in a few minutes with some saddle soap and rags. Stevie watched her as she gingerly rubbed the soap into the leather, then polished it to a soft, supple glow. Though she was careful not to chip her nails or get any dirt on her clothes, Veronica was actually doing a halfway decent job of cleaning the tack.

"Looks good," Stevie said as Veronica's pile of clean tack slowly grew.

"Hnnnh," Veronica grumped. "I thought this was what they paid people like Red O'Malley to do."

"Yes, but it's fun to learn how to do it yourself, don't you think?" Stevie replied pleasantly. If she was going to be stuck with Veronica, they might as well try to get along.

"I don't see any point in learning to do anything that you can pay somebody else to do for you," Veronica snapped. "Particularly when you're only going to do it once in your entire life."

"But you don't know that," said Stevie. "You might love driving and want to do it all the time. It looks like a lot of fun to me."

"Some of the driving costumes look fun," replied

Veronica. "I've seen pictures of great teams of horses pulling these magnificent coaches. And all the drivers and passengers are dressed in satin clothes and white wigs. And there's even a footman who rides in the rear and blows a horn to announce their arrival!"

Stevie snickered at the idea of Veronica blowing a horn to announce the Pine Hollow wagon. "I don't think we're quite ready for a horn-tooting footman. And everybody would die laughing if we showed up in satin clothes and white wigs!"

Veronica shot a look at Stevie. "Well, what had you planned on wearing for this demonstration?"

Stevie shrugged. "I thought our good show outfits would be okay."

"Our good show outfits?" Veronica rolled her eyes. "Oh, please. We've got to come up with something else. My oldest, most worn show outfit makes your very best one look like something from the rag bag. You'll only embarrass yourself if you wear it." Veronica sniffed. "You'll embarrass me, too, come to think of it."

"And just what's wrong with my good show outfit?" Stevie was suddenly so mad the tips of her ears were hot. She loved that outfit; she had worked hard babysitting to earn the money to buy it.

"Well, it's just so . . . so . . . so *prêt-à-porter*," Veronica sniffed. "Off the rack. Ready to wear. My coats and breeches are all specially tailored at Horseman's

Haberdashery in Washington." She gave Stevie an indulgent smile. "They even have a special dressmaker's dummy with my name on it."

"What an honor!" cried Stevie. She could no longer resist temptation. "Now not only one, but two dummies are named Veronica diAngelo!"

"How dare you—" Veronica's words were cut short by a muffled beep. Stevie watched as she withdrew a tiny cell phone from the pocket of her breeches. "Hello?" she said quietly, turning her back to Stevie.

Stevie started working with the tack again as Veronica got up and paced around the hallway, murmuring into the phone. Finally, as Stevie heard her say goodbye, she could have sworn Veronica's voice cracked with some kind of strong emotion. She looked up. Veronica was quickly stuffing the cell phone back in her pocket.

"I've got to go," Veronica announced, her voice like ice.

Stevie frowned. "Go? You just got here."

"I know, but something's come up. My parents are sending their car. I'll meet you here tomorrow morning."

"Well, all right," Stevie said in amazement, watching as Veronica wiped at one eye and strode off toward the locker room.

Stevie turned her attention back to the box as

Veronica disappeared down the hall. *How strange*, she thought. *Veronica shows up here to work for about five minutes, then she gets a phone call and leaves.* She stood up and looked out the window. Just as she turned to gaze out at the wide front drive, the diAngelos' white Mercedes came rolling to a stop. Stevie leaned against the window and watched. In a moment Veronica came hurrying out, once again dressed in her cashmere sweater.

"They must be having a big sale at the mall," Stevie said aloud as Veronica got into the backseat of the car. "Or maybe the Horseman's Haberdashery is having a closeout on everything that fits Veronica's dummy."

She gave a big sigh and turned back to the box of tack. She wished she were with Carole and Lisa at the library. "At least they get to be together," she grumbled out loud. "And they get to be together miles away from Veronica and her stupid dress dummy."

Oh, well, she thought as she picked up a set of blinders. Tonight she would call both of them. They would probably enjoy getting an earful about creepy Veronica, and giving it to them might make her feel a little better.

"THANKS FOR THE lift, Dad," Carole said as her father, Colonel Mitch Hanson, pulled up in front of the library. "Looks like Lisa's already here."

"Where?" Colonel Hanson steered the car close to the curb.

Carole pointed to a small figure in a red jacket. "Up there. Sitting by the lion."

"Oh, I see her." Colonel Hanson waved at Lisa as Carole unbuckled her seat belt. "Now, tell me again what you two are planning today?"

"First Lisa and I are going to work on our driving team project all morning, then Mrs. Atwood's going to take us to the mall." Carole smiled at her father as she

hopped out of the car. "I should be home around sup-
pertime."

"Sounds like fun. You guys work hard and I'll see you
later." He chuckled. "Don't buy out all the stores."

"Right, Dad, like I've got thousands of dollars to
spend!"

Carole hurried up the steps of the library, where Lisa
was waiting. "Hi," she said. "Sorry I'm late. My dad
wouldn't leave the house until he'd finished the Sunday
comics."

Lisa smiled. "Don't worry. I've only been here about
five minutes. Let's go on inside and get started. Two
weeks seems like a long time away, but it's really not."

"You're not kidding," said Carole. "We've really only
got today and whatever time we can squeeze out next
weekend. Then it'll be two weeks, and we'll be standing
in front of everybody from Horse Wise and Cross
County, too. Thank goodness the library's open Sun-
days during school or we'd *really* be in trouble!"

Lisa gave a little shudder as she opened the door. "I
know. If we aren't prepared, we'll just stand up there
and make fools of ourselves. I think we'd better get a lot
done today."

Inside, the library was just as warm and cheery as it
had been the day before. They looked around the main
reading room and saw Mrs. Davidson giving them a
friendly wave from behind the checkout desk.

"I guess we'd better go get all our reserved books," whispered Lisa.

"Okay. Let's take them to that table in the corner," Carole said as she followed Lisa to Mrs. Davidson.

"Hi, girls," chirped Mrs. Davidson. "I see you're here bright and early today."

"We've got a lot of work to do." Lisa glanced at Carole. "We didn't get quite as much done as we needed to yesterday."

Mrs. Davidson smiled. "Well, I've got all your titles on reserve. Would you like them now?"

"Yes, please," said Carole.

"I'll go get them, then." Mrs. Davidson bustled over to a small area behind the counter where several piles of books lay. She picked up about a third of Lisa and Carole's stack and lugged them back to the counter. "Here are a few. It'll take me a moment to get the rest."

"Thanks," said Carole. "We'll take these over to that table in the corner."

It took several trips, but finally Carole and Lisa had carried all forty-two books to the library table.

"How are we ever going to plow through all these pages?" Lisa wondered aloud, eyeing the stacks of books. "That's thousands of years of horse driving history, and we've only got two weeks to get it all together!"

Carole sighed. "I know. And there are so many

things we need to include, too. Like how they drove teams in the military, in transportation, and in farmwork."

"And don't forget the fun stuff," added Lisa. "Like racing and horse shows."

"I guess we'd better start reading," Carole said. "All this information isn't going to just jump inside our brains. Why don't I go sharpen our pencils while you get out our index cards?"

"Okay," said Lisa. "I'll be right here when you get back."

Carole got up and walked to the other side of the library. There was a pencil sharpener next to the children's section. She had just shoved the first pencil into the sharpener when she glanced over at a child-sized desk. A familiar little blond girl sat there, hunched over a copy of *Misty*. The book was opened to the exact place where she and Lisa had stopped reading the day before, and the little girl was tracing the illustrations with her finger.

"Cynthia!" Carole whispered. "You're here again!"

Cynthia looked up and smiled. "Hi, Carole," she greeted her shyly.

"How come you're here so early? Most people don't come to the library on Sunday mornings unless they have important research to do."

Cynthia shrugged her tiny shoulders. "Oh, I don't know," she replied. "I guess I just like it here a lot."

Carole began to sharpen her pencil. "What time did you get here?"

"Oh, right when they opened," answered Cynthia.

"And did your mother bring you?" Carole smiled.

"Yes." Cynthia looked down and rubbed a page of the book.

"Is she here?" Carole looked around to see if there were any motherly-looking women nearby.

Cynthia gave a slightly embarrassed grin and said nothing.

Suddenly Carole caught on. "She dropped you off here again, didn't she, Cynthia?"

"Well, kind of," Cynthia admitted.

"Just so she could go shopping?"

Cynthia lowered her eyes and did not reply.

"That's incredible!" Carole cried, jamming the second pencil into the sharpener and turning the crank furiously. "The idea of someone leaving a little kid here two days in a row just so she could go to the mall!" She turned to Cynthia. "You stay right here. I'll be back in a minute!"

"You're not going to tell Mrs. Davidson, are you?" Cynthia cried, a look of panic on her face.

"No," Carole said. "I promise I won't!"

53

She hurried back to where Lisa had just opened a big black book called *Horse Transport in Ancient Rome*.

"You'll never guess who I just ran into." Carole pulled out the chair next to Lisa's and sat down hard.

"I don't know." Lisa barely looked up from the pages. "Somebody from school?"

"No. Cynthia!"

"Cynthia?" Lisa looked up and blinked in amazement. "She's here again?"

Carole nodded. "Her mother has dropped her off here two days in a row! Can you imagine a parent acting like that?"

Lisa shook her head. "My mother gets pretty crazy about shopping, but she would never have dropped me off in a library all by myself. Not without a couple of armed guards, anyway." Carole nodded. She knew that Lisa's mother could sometimes be a little overprotective.

"This makes me so mad!" Carole fumed. "It's so sad to see Cynthia sitting there, just looking at the pictures of *Misty* and not being able to read a single page!"

"It is sad," agreed Lisa. "But what can we do?"

"I don't know. All I know is that Cynthia needs help. She needs to feel like somebody likes her, that she's not just a pest to be dropped off somewhere on the way to the mall." Carole chewed her thumbnail for a moment, then looked at Lisa, her brown eyes sparkling.

"I just had a great idea! I know we've got all this research to do, but it doesn't mean we have to do it together, all the time. Why don't we take turns? One of us can work on the history of driving while the other reads *Misty* to Cynthia."

"Okay," agreed Lisa. "That way she won't feel like such an outcast, and at least one of us will be getting some work done."

Carole frowned. "Pretty soon we'll have to come up with a way to get her mother to quit doing this altogether, but for now I can't think of a better thing to do than to make this little girl feel special."

"I think you're right. Let's start this minute," said Lisa. "Do you want to read first or do research?"

"You read first," replied Carole. "I'll get started on this."

"Great," Lisa said. "Let's go tell Cynthia."

"Wait." Carole scooted back in the chair. "Don't let her know how upset we are about her mother. That'll only make her feel worse than she already does."

"Okay."

Lisa and Carole walked back to where Cynthia was still tracing over the pony illustrations.

"Hi, Cynthia," Lisa said as she and Carole sat down at the tiny table. "Want to read some more of *Misty*?"

Cynthia looked up at them, her blue eyes wide.

55

"Sure I do. But aren't you two working on some school project?"

"Well, we decided to take turns," explained Carole. "We had such a good time reading to you yesterday that we thought we could at least read a little bit more today."

Cynthia beamed. "But we won't read anywhere near Mrs. Davidson, will we? She almost saw me this morning when she was getting a huge stack of books from behind the counter. I had to run to the back of the children's section as fast as I could."

Carole and Lisa shared a guilty look. The only reserve books Mrs. Davidson had doled out that morning had been their own stack. "Oh, no," Carole reassured Cynthia. "We'll stay far away from Mrs. Davidson."

"Okay," Cynthia agreed excitedly.

"Let's go find a quiet corner," Lisa said. "I'll read the next couple of chapters, then Carole and I will switch off and she can read."

"That sounds like fun!" said Cynthia.

They got up from the table and walked toward a little nook in the wall, close to the reserved book counter.

"What's your mother like, Cynthia?" Lisa asked as they squeezed between two tall bookcases.

"She's real pretty and sweet," Cynthia said, smiling.

56

"She let me adopt a kitten from the animal shelter, and she pops me popcorn and reads lots of books to me when we're at home."

Carole was curious. "What does she like to buy at the mall?"

"Red pocketbooks," Cynthia giggled. "She has a whole collection of them. They're all great big and she carries them over her shoulder. People tease her about them all the time."

They reached the little nook, which was empty. Lisa and Cynthia sat down together on the floor. Carole smiled. "Well, I guess I'll go back to our work. Come and get me when it's my turn, Lisa."

"Right." Lisa opened the book to where they'd stopped the day before. "See you in a little while."

Carole turned and had begun to retrace her steps toward their table when she saw Mrs. Davidson heading for the reserved books. An elderly woman followed close behind. For an instant Carole panicked. If they kept going straight, they would certainly see Lisa and Cynthia. Carole hurried toward them.

"Hi, Mrs. Davidson," she called loudly. "Anything I can help you with?"

"No, dear, I was just going to get Mrs. Lovejoy her books on mushrooms."

"Mushrooms?" Carole cried. "Really? I love to read

about mushrooms! Why don't you let me get Mrs. Lovejoy's books? That way I can have a peek at them before I get back to my own work."

Mrs. Lovejoy smiled while Mrs. Davidson just looked confused. "Well, uh, I guess that would be all right. If you don't mind, that is."

"No, no," said Carole. "I'd love to!"

She waited for Mrs. Davidson to turn back to the checkout desk, then hurriedly picked up Mrs. Lovejoy's mushroom books and deposited them on the table she'd chosen.

"Don't you want to look at them first, dear?" said Mrs. Lovejoy.

"Uh, maybe later," said Carole, who was watching Mrs. Davidson at the checkout desk again. She was talking to a man and pointing in Lisa and Cynthia's direction. "Right now I've got to help Mrs. Davidson."

She hurried back up to the counter. "All the Italian dictionaries are located just this side of that big globe," Mrs. Davidson was telling the man. "If you follow me, I'll be happy to show you where."

"Uh, did you say Italian dictionaries, Mrs. Davidson?" Carole leaned forward.

Mrs. Davidson blinked with even more surprise, then nodded. "Why, yes, dear. This gentleman needs to translate a letter."

"I'd be happy to show him where they are," Carole

blurted out. She shrugged. "I mean, it's on my way back to my table, and I look at the Italian dictionaries a lot. I'm going to take Italian when I get to high school. I might even go live in Italy someday."

Mrs. Davidson looked mystified. "Well, of course, if you're sure you know where they are."

"Oh, I do." Carole turned and smiled at the man. "Just follow me, sir."

She led the man to the dictionaries, deciding that it wasn't exactly a fib she'd just told. She supposed she could take Italian once she got to high school, although she really hadn't given it a single thought. She snuck a quick glance at Lisa and Cynthia reading away as she passed. *Thank heavens*, she thought. *So far, so good.*

After she pointed out all the Italian dictionaries, she helped Mrs. Davidson pull some medical reference books for a man with a broken finger; then she helped a little girl find an aerial map of Peru. By the time she got back to the table to start researching the history of driving, Lisa was waiting to take over.

"Hi," Lisa said. "I've finished my chapters. How far have you gotten?"

"Not far at all," said Carole, almost out of breath. "Every time I turn around, Mrs. Davidson is either about to lead someone past that little nook or she's looking something up for somebody. I've spent the whole time keeping her away from you and Cynthia!"

"What should we do?" Lisa asked.

"Well, I'll go read. You do as much research as you can, but keep an eye on Mrs. Davidson. She buzzes around here like a bee!"

"Okay," Lisa promised.

Carole walked over to the nook and sat down beside Cynthia. As she read the next two chapters of *Misty*, she stayed on the lookout for the librarian. Apparently Lisa was doing the same thing. Once Carole saw her shelving some books in the cookbook section; then she saw her hurrying to take a young couple over to the periodicals. As Carole neared the end of her chapters, Lisa was looking up information on butterflies for a couple of Brownies. Mrs. Davidson, though, had not left the checkout desk. Carole gave a big sigh and looked at her watch. It was time to go. They'd spent all morning at the library, and as far as she could tell, all they'd done was help other people out in the reference room and read several chapters of *Misty* to Cynthia.

Lisa appeared. "Carole, have you checked the time?"

Carole nodded. "I know. We've got to go." She looked over at Cynthia. "I'm sorry we can't stay and read more of *Misty*, Cynthia, but we've got to go now. We promised Lisa's mom we'd be at her house before one."

"That's okay." Cynthia's voice sagged with disappointment. "You were great to read to me. I'll just go

60

back to my secret hiding place and look at the pictures for the rest of the afternoon."

"We hate to leave you," said Lisa. "Are you sure you'll be okay till your mom comes?"

Cynthia gathered up her book and nodded. "I guess so," she replied sadly. Then she looked up, happier. "My mom said she might come back early this afternoon and take me to the mall!"

"That would be wonderful, Cynthia," said Carole as she got to her feet. "I hope she does, and I hope you have a great time."

"Thanks," said Cynthia with a wan smile. "Bye," she called as she scurried off into the dark corners of the stacks.

Carole and Lisa walked slowly over to their table. "Can you believe we've been here all morning and haven't taken one note?" asked Lisa. "We could have gotten so much more done if we'd just thought to move Cynthia to a different location."

"I know," agreed Carole. "But everything started happening so fast. It seemed like every time I looked up, Mrs. Davidson was on her way to that little nook!"

"Carole, we've got to do something about this," said Lisa as she zipped up her jacket. "We can't just let Cynthia's mother keep on leaving her here like this. Even if she does come pick her up early this afternoon, it's still practically child abandonment!"

"I know." Carole tied her scarf snugly around her neck. "Let's give it some thought on the way to your house. Maybe we'll have some brilliant flash of inspiration."

"We need Stevie," Lisa said. "When it comes to brilliant flashes of inspiration, she's the one to have on your team!"

"MORNING, GIRL," STEVIE said softly. "How about a good scratch behind your ears?"

Belle stepped forward in her stall. Though she had already been fed, it was barely eight o'clock on Sunday morning, and she had the same sleepy look in her eyes that Stevie did.

"I bet you're surprised to see me here so early," Stevie whispered as she rubbed Belle's soft ears. "I'm surprised to be here myself, but I've got to work on our project today, and who knows when my wonderful partner will show up. She's probably having breakfast with her French friends, and you know how the French are about breakfast!" Stevie imitated Veronica's haughty voice as Belle flicked her ears in surprise.

63

"I gotta go now." She gave the horse a final pat. "I'll see you in a little while."

She turned down the hall and began to walk toward the back storage room, where she'd stashed the driving tack she'd untangled the day before. As she turned the corner, she noticed a light on in Danny's stall and a wheelbarrow of dirty straw sitting by the door. She walked over and peeked inside, then gasped. In the middle of the stall, dressed in a sweatshirt and jeans, stood Veronica diAngelo!

"Veronica!" Stevie's voice came out in a surprised croak. "What are you doing here?"

Veronica turned and gave her an icy stare. "What does it look like I'm doing? I've just cleaned Danny's stall, and now I'm grooming him."

"B-But it's so early in the morning," Stevie stuttered. "I didn't think you'd get here before noon."

"Looks like you thought wrong, didn't you?" Veronica smirked over her shoulder.

For a moment Stevie was so astonished, she couldn't think of anything to say. Then she decided that since Veronica had actually shown up, they'd better get some work done. "Well, I'm glad to see you. I finished cleaning the rest of the tack yesterday afternoon, so I guess we should start working the horses together. Why don't we take Danny and Belle out to the back paddock and longe them together in the driving harness?"

Veronica frowned for a moment, then shrugged. "Oh, all right," she finally muttered. "You set it up. I'll bring the horses."

"Okay." Stevie smiled. Even though Veronica was not in the sunniest of moods, at least she seemed to be willing to cooperate a little. Stevie headed to the storage room and fished the proper pieces of tack out of the box. Then she grabbed an extra-long longe line and headed to the back paddock. She had just checked to make sure she had two sets of each piece of tack when Veronica led Danny into the paddock.

"We're ready," Veronica announced, standing impatiently with one hand on her hip.

Stevie looked up and frowned. "Where's Belle?"

"I don't know. In her stall, I suppose," snapped Veronica.

"You were supposed to bring her out, too, Veronica. A team of horses implies that there will be more than one horse."

"So?"

Stevie felt her face heating up with anger. "So go get Belle now, like you promised, while I finish with this tack."

"Oh, whatever." Veronica unclipped Danny's lead

line and walked slowly back to the stable. A few moments later she came out with Belle walking beside her. "Here's your beast, Stevie," she said, flipping the lead rope in Stevie's direction.

"Thanks," Stevie muttered, giving Belle a reassuring pat on the neck. *If there's any beast in this paddock*, she thought, *it walks on two legs and answers to the name of Veronica.* She took a deep breath and whispered the word *patience* three times.

"Why don't we try to get them into this harness first?" Stevie suggested. "All this stuff needs to fit properly." She held up one bridle. "This goes on the horse who pulls on the right."

"Well, that will have to be Belle," Veronica sniffed.

"Why?" asked Stevie.

"Because the left horse is the lead horse, and Danny needs to be the lead horse."

"Why?" Stevie asked again.

"Because he's high-strung. He needs to lead."

Stevie frowned. "If he's that high-strung, maybe he should follow. He might spook being in the lead."

"If he's not in the lead, he probably won't pull at all," Veronica warned.

"He can't help but pull, if Belle's in the lead and she's pulling, too."

"It doesn't work like that." Veronica turned her mouth down in a stubborn line.

66

"How do you know? How many wagons have you driven?"

Veronica's green eyes flashed. "About as many as you have."

Stevie took another deep breath and whispered *patience* again. "Well, why don't we just try longeing them together like this and see what happens?"

"I don't see the point in longeing them if they aren't going to pull the wagon in the same way."

"Well, then, let's get the rest of the tack adjusted on them," Stevie suggested. "Then we can decide who pulls where."

"Oh, all right." Veronica walked over and looked at the tack Stevie had cleaned. She picked through it, choosing the best pieces for Danny and leaving the more worn bits for Belle.

"Hey!" cried Stevie. "Let's divide this up more equally. It's not fair for Danny to have all the best pieces."

"Why not?" asked Veronica. "He's obviously the best horse."

Stevie opened her mouth to give Veronica a large dose of her opinion about Danny when Max's voice rang out.

"Veronica!" he called, cupping his hands around his mouth. "You've got a call in the office! They said it was important."

67

"Thanks," Veronica replied. She tossed Danny's lead rope to Stevie. "Here. You can hold him till I get back."

Seething with anger, Stevie watched as Veronica hurried into the stable and Max sauntered over to the fence.

"How's it going?" he asked.

Stevie led both horses over to him. "Max, Veronica has just hit a new low in being the most obnoxious person at this stable. She won't cooperate over anything. Danny has to lead. Danny has to have the best tack. Danny can't be bothered with longeing with Belle. I don't think this partnership is going to work!"

"Oh, I bet it can," Max replied calmly.

"No, it won't. Not when Veronica acts like the biggest, most stubborn jerk who's ever pulled on riding boots!" Stevie's voice rose so high that Belle jumped.

"Well, did you ever think it might not be much fun to be Veronica? You don't know what's going on in her life right now." Max frowned at her. "Stevie, you shouldn't judge people until you've ridden a mile in their boots."

"I wouldn't ride a mile in her custom-made boots even if I could!" cried Stevie. "They'd probably cut off my circulation!"

"Well, you two work it out." Max patted Stevie on the shoulder and walked back to his office.

"I'll do my best," Stevie whispered as she led the horses back to the center of the paddock.

She fit the bridle and blinders on Belle first, then worked on Danny. He was as cooperative as his owner was uncooperative. Just as Stevie made the final adjustments on his tack, Veronica walked back into the paddock.

"Hi," Stevie began. "I gave Danny the better bit, and Belle the better—"

Veronica wasn't listening. She walked directly over to Danny and wrapped her arms around his neck, burying her face in his dapple gray coat and giving him a long, affectionate hug.

Stevie's mouth fell open. She'd never seen Veronica display any kind of affection toward any animal, ever. She almost turned away, embarrassed, but then Veronica let go of Danny and looked at Stevie. Again Stevie's jaw dropped. She could have sworn she saw actual tears in Veronica's eyes. She shook her head. *You must be dreaming,* she told herself. *You got up way too early this morning and you're still dreaming. Only people who have hearts cry, and all Veronica has inside her chest is some kind of weird pump made of eighteen-carat gold.*

Still, they looked like real tears glistening in her eyes. "Veronica?" Stevie asked softly.

"Let's get to work." Veronica briskly turned her back

to Stevie. "Danny's very smart. He gets bored just standing around doing nothing."

"Okay," agreed Stevie. "Let's see if they'll longe together."

"Only if Danny can be on the left," insisted Veronica.

"Fine." Stevie gave up and clipped the right end of the checkrein to Belle's bridle. *Being upset enough to cry sure doesn't make her easier to get along with*, she thought as Veronica fumbled with the longe line.

Finally they got the line sorted out and walked to the center of the paddock. "Here," Veronica said. "Give the line to me. I want to drive first."

Stevie handed the longe line to Veronica and stood back to watch. Veronica cracked the long driving whip loudly and clucked to both horses. Belle started out at a trot, but Danny immediately leaped into a canter. They bumped halfway around the paddock, knocking into each other at both turns.

"Slow them down, Veronica," warned Stevie. "Or at least get them both in the same gait."

"I know what I'm doing," Veronica said. "This is the way Danny likes to get started."

"But Belle doesn't know what to do," cried Stevie.

"Well, that's obvious. Belle's certainly not the horse Danny is. I wonder if she's even fit to pull a wagon with him." Veronica cracked the whip again.

"She's every bit the horse Danny is," Stevie retorted. "Maybe even more."

The horses continued around the paddock. Veronica's constant cracking of the whip made Belle shift to a canter. That gave Danny the idea that they were racing. As Belle cantered past, he dipped his head and nipped at her shoulder. Belle gave a high whinny of pain and reared back, pawing at Danny with her front hooves.

"Veronica!" Stevie cried. "Stop them!"

"I can't!" Veronica screamed, dropping the longe line completely.

Now both horses were out of control. Belle reared up again, trying to hit Danny with her hooves. Danny's head darted low as he snapped at Belle's legs. Finally he twisted the longe line and wedged himself sideways behind Belle and started kicking at the paddock fence with his powerful back legs.

"Stop it, Danny! Stop it!" Veronica shrieked. "You're going to get killed!"

Stevie didn't know what to do. She knew it was dangerous to get between two angry, out-of-control horses, but if she didn't do something fast they were both going to get badly hurt. She ran across the paddock and grabbed the longe line that held them together. She unclipped Belle, who raced to the other side of the paddock, and then she put all her weight on Danny's

71

line, forcing him to stop kicking and stand on all four legs. Both horses were streaked with sweat, and their ears were slapped back against their skulls.

"Hey, what's going on here?"

Stevie looked around to see Max leaping over the paddock fence. "Is everything okay?"

"I think it is now," replied Stevie, breathing hard. She was so scared she was shaking.

"What happened?" Max demanded, scowling with concern.

"Veronica got them going too fast," gasped Stevie. "Danny thought they were racing and tried to bite Belle. Then she freaked out."

Max frowned at Stevie, then at Veronica. "Look, girls. I don't intend to have either of these horses injured over this project. Are you two sure you're mature enough to handle this?"

"I certainly am." Veronica picked up the driving whip. "And so is Danny. It's just Belle. She's such an obviously inferior horse of mixed breeding."

"No, she's not, Veronica," Max replied sternly. "Belle is an intelligent animal with a lot of heart. Anyway, it's not the horses I'm worried about. I thought you and Stevie were up to this challenge, but maybe I gave you too much credit."

"We're sorry, Max," Stevie apologized. She glanced at Veronica. "I know we can do this safely. I think we just need to work on our communication skills a little bit."

"Are you sure?" Max sounded unconvinced.

Stevie nodded. "Give us one more chance. We'll do it right. We promise."

"Okay," Max said, relenting. "One more chance. But if I hear as much as a whinny from this paddock, the only thing you two are going to be allowed to do at that joint meeting is hand out cookies and lemonade."

"Yes, sir." Stevie looked at the ground as her dream of triumph disappeared. This was hopeless. Veronica was going to do everything she could to blow Stevie's chance at impressing Phil at that meeting. Phil had even been hinting that he was going to do something special for the show, and here was her only big chance to do something even more special, and this idiotic girl was going to spoil it. They would be relegated to handing out cookies with the D-level Pony Clubbers, and it would all be Veronica's fault. Stevie stood silently with her fists clenched until Max disappeared into the barn. Then she turned to Veronica.

"How dare you imply that my horse has inferior breeding!" Stevie cried. "She's got Arabian blood, mixed with some Saddlebred, and that makes the best combination in the world. She's kind, she's smart, and who would blame her for rearing up when another, bigger bully of a horse tried to bite her? She was just defending herself! Anyway, Veronica, you wouldn't know good breeding if it bit you on the nose. If anyone in this paddock suffers from a rotten pedigree, it's you!"

Stevie glared at Veronica for a moment, waiting for her reply. But instead of pulling herself up into her usual haughty stance, Veronica seemed to sag. She covered her face with both hands and burst into tears, crying as if her heart were breaking.

For a moment Stevie didn't know what to say. She still felt angry, but she'd never seen Veronica shed a single tear, much less burst into loud sobs. "Veronica?" she finally asked. "What's going on?"

"You wouldn't understand," Veronica sobbed.

"Yes I would," Stevie said more softly. "Try me."

"No you wouldn't." Veronica gave a loud sniff.

"Yes I would," Stevie insisted.

"You wouldn't care, anyway," Veronica said in a thick voice.

"I might care a lot if you'd tell me." Stevie took a step toward her.

Veronica looked up and wiped the tears from her eyes. She gave a resigned sigh. "You know that phone call I got yesterday?"

Stevie nodded.

"That was my mother telling me that she had to take our little white poodle, Robespierre, to the vet. He's only six years old, and he's got a champion pedigree

74

and he's a wonderful dog. The vet thinks it's serious—
he had to stay in the animal hospital last night." Veronica teared up again. "I'm just so afraid he's going to
die!"

"Oh, Veronica, it's probably not that bad." Stevie
figured the dog had probably just gotten into the di-
Angelos' caviar when they weren't looking and Veronica was milking it for all it was worth.

"And just a few minutes ago, Dr. Takamura called
and said that Robespierre was in a lot of pain, and we
need to think about putting him to sleep!" Veronica
began to weep again.

"Oh, no," Stevie said softly. Now she knew Veronica
wasn't kidding. If Doc Tock called and said that, little
Robespierre must really be in bad shape. "I'm so sorry,
Veronica. Why don't you go sit on that bale of hay? I'll
get the harness off the horses."

"Okay." Veronica said, sniffling.

Stevie unhooked Belle and Danny from their driving
tack and tied them to the fence near Veronica. They
seemed to have forgotten their fight—both were con-
tent to munch on some hay in the paddock, side by side.

Stevie walked over and sat down next to Veronica.
She'd stopped crying, but her nose was red and her eyes
puffy.

"Are you feeling a little better?" Stevie asked sympa-
thetically.

Veronica nodded. "It always helps to talk to someone. Especially someone who knows about animals. Sometimes I don't think my parents understand."

"I know what you mean." Stevie smiled. "I know my brothers think I'm crazy for loving Belle like I do."

"Sometimes I think when I'm grown up and have my own money, I'll buy a lot of horses. You know, mistreated ones, and just let them run around my big farm and have a good time."

"That would be a great thing to do," Stevie agreed.

"My father would think I was crazy," Veronica said. "He thinks I'm crazy to be so upset about Robespierre."

"It's always sad when a pet is sick," Stevie replied. "But Doc Tock is the best vet around. She won't let Robespierre suffer. And who knows, maybe Robespierre will recover. You never know about these things. It's important not to lose hope."

"I know." Veronica leaned over and gave Stevie a sweet smile. "You're absolutely right."

A soft beep echoed through the air. Veronica dug in her pocket and pulled out her cell phone.

"Hello?" she said. Stevie couldn't help overhearing the call. It was obviously Veronica's mother, and the subject was Robespierre.

"Great," said Veronica. "I'll be out front in ten minutes." She switched off the phone and smiled again at Stevie. "That was my mother. Dr. Takamura says

Robespierre's condition has stabilized and he can have visitors. Mom's going to pick me up and we're going over there to see him." Her eyes clouded up again. "I only hope it won't be for the—the last time."

Stevie reached over and squeezed Veronica's shoulder. "Don't think like that. Just keep your thoughts positive."

"I'll try." Veronica stood up. "That's just what I need to do. Well, I guess I'd better hurry."

She gave Stevie a brief smile, then ran back to the stable, leaving Stevie sitting alone on the hay bale with the two munching horses. For a while Stevie just stayed there, thinking that Veronica was really very nice on the inside and she and Carole and Lisa had never known it. *Maybe we should have tried to really talk to her years ago,* Stevie thought. *Maybe we could have all been good friends.* Suddenly Stevie's stomach growled. It was way past lunchtime, and also past time to put Danny and Belle back in their stalls.

She stood up. Veronica was long gone, and nobody else was in sight. She was going to have to take care of Danny and Belle all by herself. "Oh well," she said as she untied the horses from the fence. "So what if I have to do a little extra work? Veronica's got a lot on her mind, and I certainly don't mind doing a favor for someone with a troubled heart!"

"I STILL CAN'T believe anybody would do that to a five-year-old girl," Carole fumed. She and Lisa were walking toward Lisa's house. Though the temperature was cold, sunlight sparkled in the blue sky.

"I know." Lisa stuffed her hands deep in her jacket pockets. "It makes me angry just to think about it. Sometimes you hear about stuff like that on the news, but when it happens right in front of you, it seems unreal."

"And Mrs. Davidson!" Carole continued. "She's so nice and sweet and helpful to us. How could she possibly consider throwing that little girl out on the street? Particularly on a day like yesterday, when it was so rainy and miserable?"

"It couldn't be her," said Lisa. "Maybe her boss is mean and makes her do it. I'm sure the library has rules, just like everyplace else."

"Well, it seems like she could bend the rules in a case like this," muttered Carole. "I mean, Cynthia's only five. It's not like she's got a lot of choice in the matter."

Lisa gave a big sigh. "Well, we've done the best we could to make her feel better. We've read most of *Misty* to her, and we've tried to make her feel good about herself."

Carole pushed back a lock of dark curly hair that had fallen into her eyes and looked seriously at Lisa. "I think we should tell some grown-up about this."

Lisa frowned. "Like who?"

"I don't know," said Carole. "Maybe your mom. Or my dad."

"Or we could explain it all to Mrs. Davidson," Lisa suggested. "Or we could even call the police."

Carole shook her head. "I don't think so. They might take Cynthia away from her mother. And nothing she's ever said about her mom has been bad."

"That's right," Lisa said. "Cynthia thinks her mother is great. She says she takes her to the movies and lets her friends come over for sleepovers and fixes pancakes for them on Saturday mornings." She shrugged. "She sounds like a great mom."

"Except for one tiny flaw," replied Carole. "She just

can't quit leaving Cynthia at the library while she goes to shop at the mall!"

"Maybe we should try to talk to her," Lisa suggested. "Maybe we should wait for her at the library someday when she picks Cynthia up. Then we could tell her that she has to stop, or else we'll tell the police."

"But we can't wait for Cynthia's mother at the library every day," said Carole.

Lisa stopped in her tracks. "Wait! I've got the perfect plan!"

Carole's brown eyes grew wide. "What?"

"Mom's taking us over to the mall this afternoon anyway, to shop at that big sale. We can look for Cynthia's mom there!"

Carole grinned. "That's a great idea! Cynthia said her mom always carries a big red pocketbook over her right shoulder. How many women do that? Probably not more than two or three. We could find her and talk to her and convince her that she needs to quit stashing her daughter in the stacks. Lisa, you're a genius!"

Lisa laughed. "Maybe I've just hung around Stevie long enough to have some of that brilliant inspiration of hers rub off on me!"

They turned down the driveway to Lisa's house. Inside, Mrs. Atwood had a hot lunch of vegetable soup and grilled cheese sandwiches waiting for them.

"I'm delighted that you're coming with us, Carole,"

said Mrs. Atwood with a smile. "But I never thought you were particularly interested in shopping."

"Oh, sometimes I am," Carole said with a secret grin at Lisa. "I guess it just depends on what I'm shopping for."

The girls finished their lunch quickly and helped Mrs. Atwood with the dishes. Soon they all piled into the car, heading for the huge mall on the outskirts of town. When Mrs. Atwood pulled into the parking lot, it was already packed with cars.

"Looks like everybody's come to shop today," said Mrs. Atwood. Carole and Lisa looked at each other and winked.

They parked as close as they could get to the store where Mrs. Atwood wanted to shop, then began to trudge toward the store between the parked cars. Carole and Lisa looked for a woman with a red pocketbook over her shoulder, but all they saw was a couple pushing a baby stroller and two teenagers on skateboards.

"No luck so far," whispered Carole.

"We'll do better when we get inside," replied Lisa with a grin.

They walked into the main department store. It seemed that everyone in Willow Creek was there, trying on shoes or holding up scarves or squirting themselves with samples of perfume.

"Let's go up to the junior department," said Mrs.

Atwood. "Lisa, you need practically a whole new winter wardrobe this year."

Lisa rolled her eyes at Carole, but they both followed Mrs. Atwood up the escalator. All the while they looked for a woman with a big red pocketbook, but the store was so crowded and Mrs. Atwood was moving so fast that they had little time to study the crowd.

"Okay," said Mrs. Atwood as they walked into the junior department. "First we'll start with sweaters, then we'll try on some jeans; then, Lisa, I want you to look at a dress or two."

"Oh, Mom, no dresses today," Lisa groaned. "Please?"

"Well, let's start with sweaters first and then see how you feel."

Mrs. Atwood led them over to a display of cardigans. "How about this?" She held up a pretty green sweater. "It would go well with your eyes."

"Yeah, that's fine, Mom," Lisa said distractedly, looking over toward the children's department.

"Or how about this pretty pink one? That would complement your complexion."

"Uh-huh." Lisa was scanning the toy department.

"Or even this peach-colored one. Peach is such a flattering color." When Lisa didn't answer, Mrs. Atwood looked around. Both girls were staring over into the pots and pans.

82

Mrs. Atwood frowned. "Lisa? What's going on with you two today? Your attention seems to be everywhere but where it's supposed to be."

"Sorry, Mom," Lisa said quickly, glancing at the sweaters. "That one's fine."

"Which one?" asked Mrs. Atwood. "The green, the pink, or the peach?"

"Oh, the green. It's great. I love it." Lisa looked at her mother and smiled. "Mom, I think Carole and I are going over to the adult department."

"The adult department?" Mrs. Atwood looked mystified. "Whatever for?"

"I don't know. I think they had some nice . . . nice . . . uh, pocketbooks over there," Lisa said. "Why don't we meet you back here a little later?"

Mrs. Atwood blinked. "But what about picking out your clothes? We came here especially to shop for you today."

"Oh, Mom, anything you like will be fine," said Lisa. "You usually make all my choices, anyway."

"Well, okay." Mrs. Atwood watched in amazement as the two girls hurried off to the handbag department.

"You don't think we made her mad, do you?" Carole asked as they headed around a display of fuzzy stuffed animals with music boxes in their stomachs.

"No," said Lisa. "I think we surprised her. But she'll

have a good time. There's nothing she likes better than picking out clothes for me."

"Have you seen any likely suspects for Cynthia's mother?" Carole asked as they hurried down the aisle.

"I thought I saw a lady browsing over this way," said Lisa. "Let's go over here and see if we can find her again. Remember, we need to look for a lady who could have a five-year-old child and who carries a red pocketbook on her right shoulder."

They scurried over to the women's shoe department. There, looking over a table of slippers, stood a woman wearing a hooded car coat, with a big red pocketbook on her right shoulder.

"Look," Carole whispered. "That might be her."

Lisa frowned. "Let's go over and see."

The girls inched their way down the table, pretending to look at the shoes. Finally they stood next to the woman. Lisa reached over and tapped her on the shoulder.

"Excuse me, ma'am," she said.

"Yes?" The woman turned. Lisa caught her breath. The lady had snow white hair and twinkling blue eyes. She was more likely to be Cynthia's great-grandmother than her mother.

"Uh, have you seen any snow boots on this table?" Lisa asked quickly.

"No. But I believe you can find them down in sporting goods," the woman said kindly.

"That's right," said Lisa. "I wasn't thinking. Thanks!"

She and Carole turned quickly away from the shoe table. "Well, so much for that red pocketbook," said Carole. She stood on her toes and looked around the store. "See anyone else?"

"Yes," cried Lisa. "There's a woman with a red pocketbook over there trying on earrings, and there's another one heading out into the mall."

"And there's one over there buying perfume," said Carole. She frowned at Lisa. "Suddenly it seems like half the women in this mall have red pocketbooks on their shoulders."

"This might be harder than we thought," said Lisa. "But we've got to try. Think of poor little Cynthia all alone at the library, hiding from Mrs. Davidson!"

They walked over to the woman buying perfume. She was the right age, but she spoke broken English with a thick Spanish accent, and her hair was dark and curly.

"I don't think that's Cynthia mother," whispered Carole. "They don't look anything alike, and I think Cynthia would have told us if her mother was from another country."

"You're right," said Lisa. "Let's move on to that woman in the jewelry department."

The woman trying on earrings had just opened her pocketbook to pay for her jewelry. As Carole and Lisa approached, three redheaded children ran up. They were all about five years old, were dressed alike, and looked exactly alike.

"Mama! Mama!" they all cried together. "Can we go get a cookie at the cookie stand?"

The woman looked down and smiled at them. "Alison, Abigail, and Alexandra, have you all behaved yourselves while I shopped?"

The little girls nodded. "Yes, Mama," they said in unison.

"Well," the woman laughed, "I guess you can have a cookie, then. Let me pay for these earrings and we'll go. Everybody hold hands, though, so you won't get lost."

The little girls all held hands and soon followed the woman out into the mall, like little ducklings waddling after their mother.

Carole and Lisa looked at each other in astonishment. "They're triplets!" Lisa cried.

"That's right," said the salesclerk. "That's Mrs. Mc-Elroy. She shops here every weekend and brings them all with her. Aren't they precious?"

"They sure are." Carole smiled, then looked at Lisa. "So much for Mrs. McElroy."

"Let's go out into the mall. Maybe we'll have better luck out there."

They went out into the mall. It, too, was crowded with shoppers. As Carole and Lisa studied the throngs of people moving from store to store, it seemed that hundreds of women had red pocketbooks slung over their shoulders.

"Wow!" exclaimed Carole. "I had no idea red bags were so popular."

"Me neither," said Lisa. "I guess the best thing we can do is keep looking and asking the people who most fit the description of Cynthia's mother."

They walked up and down the mall, paying particular attention to women's clothing stores and shoe stores.

When Carole remembered that Cynthia had said her mother bought her lots of things, they started looking in stores that specialized in items for children. Lots of women were out shopping with big red pocketbooks, but few looked like they could be Cynthia's mother. One woman was perfect, except she was visiting Willow Creek from Boise, Idaho. Another good candidate was moving to Tampa, Florida, and had sent her children on ahead of her. As Carole and Lisa neared one end of the mall, they looked at each and sighed.

"You know what this reminds me of?" asked Carole, frowning with frustration.

"Looking for a needle in a haystack?" Lisa replied dispiritedly.

"Exactly," replied Carole. "Only the needle has a big red pocketbook."

"Yeah, along with about every other woman in Willow Creek. It wouldn't surprise me now if my own mother came walking up with one." Lisa shook her head. "So much for my brilliant flash of inspiration."

"We need Stevie here now," said Carole. "I bet she could think of something."

The girls walked on. Suddenly Lisa stopped. "Look!" she cried. "In the BonTon gift shop!"

"Cynthia's mother?" Carole's eyes were wide with excitement.

"No," said Lisa. "But I could have sworn it was Stevie!"

"In the BonTon gift shop?" Carole frowned. "Stevie barely has enough money to buy ice cream at TD's. There's no way she could afford anything at BonTon."

"I know, but it looked just like her," Lisa insisted.

"Well, let's go see," said Carole. "If we can find Stevie in an expensive gift shop, we can find anyone anywhere."

8

STEVIE LOOKED UP in surprise from the glittering display she had been examining. "Lisa!" she cried. "Carole! I thought you guys were at the library."

"We were, until lunchtime. Then Lisa's mom brought us over here," explained Carole. She looked at the display in front of Stevie. All sorts of beautiful little china figurines gleamed down from the shelves. "How come you're here looking at little china animals?"

"Little *expensive* china animals?" Lisa added, checking the price tag on one tiny peacock.

"You won't believe me." Stevie put the white china dog she'd been considering back on the shelf. "Not in a million years."

"Try us," said Carole. "After our adventures in the library, we'd probably believe anything."

"You know how Veronica's been even meaner and nastier than her usual mean and nasty self lately?"

Lisa and Carole nodded.

"Well, there's actually a good reason for it," Stevie said.

"Of course there is," answered Lisa. "She's genetically programmed to be a thoroughly rotten human being. She can't help it."

"No, listen," Stevie said, her hazel eyes serious. "Veronica's dog, Robespierre, is really sick. She's gotten three calls about him since we've been working on the team driving project. Two were from her mother, I think, but the other was from Doc Tock herself."

"Doc Tock called?" The smile faded from Carole's face. "Then it really must be serious."

Stevie nodded. "She doesn't know if the dog is going to make it or not. Veronica's really upset. She actually cried this morning."

"Veronica diAngelo?" Lisa asked in amazement. "Cried real tears?"

"She hugged Danny's neck in the paddock and cried," Stevie reported. "I feel so sorry for her, I just want to do something to make her feel better. After I finished up at the stable, I took the bus out here. I thought maybe a china dog that looked like Robespierre might cheer her up." Stevie touched the little dog she'd just been looking at. "This one's perfect, but it costs about three times more than I've got to spend."

"That's terrible about her dog," said Carole. "I know how awful I would feel if anything happened to my cat, Snowball."

Lisa looked sad, too. "I don't know what I would do if our dog, Dolly, got sick."

"I think anyone who loves horses can sympathize when something bad happens to any kind of animal." Tears brimmed in Stevie's eyes. "I just wish I could buy this and make Veronica feel better."

"If you think that little china dog will make Veronica feel better about Robespierre, then maybe we should all pitch in and buy it," Carole said.

Lisa's jaw dropped in astonishment. "Buy Veronica diAngelo a gift? Guys, she's barely civil to us. She's never been nice at all, and she's always getting us into trouble. Plus, that dog costs as much as a whole month of sundaes at TD's."

"I know it's not logical," Carole admitted. "But these are not logical circumstances."

"Right," agreed Stevie. "Normally we wouldn't dream of buying Veronica anything, but normally her dog isn't dying."

"Well, I guess I can relate to that," Lisa said. "Count me in. Why don't we make it a joint gift from The Saddle Club?"

"Great idea!" Stevie gently lifted the little dog from the shelf and carefully took it over to the checkout counter.

They pooled their money and paid for the dog, and, after the clerk had gift-wrapped it in the gift shop's famous silver wrapping paper, they returned to the throng of shoppers in the mall.

"Okay," said Stevie, holding Veronica's gift tightly under her arm. "Now tell me why you guys are here and not at the library."

"We're looking for women with red pocketbooks over their right shoulders," said Lisa.

Stevie frowned. "Huh?"

"Red pocketbooks," repeated Carole. "Stevie, you wouldn't believe this little girl we met at the library." The three girls sat down on a bench, and Carole and Lisa filled Stevie in on Cynthia. They told her how Cynthia's mother left her at the library almost every day; how Mrs. Davidson was nice to them but threatened to throw Cynthia out into the cold November rain; and how for the past two days they'd done nothing but read *Misty* to Cynthia and try to keep Mrs. Davidson from finding out.

"Wow," said Stevie. "No wonder you're looking for

her mother. How on earth are you going to get your report done for Max if you don't find her?"

"I don't know," said Lisa. "And I'm beginning to get really nervous about it. We don't have a lot of time left."

"Well then, let's split up and look for her. Three heads are always better than two," Stevie said, glancing around the mall. "Let's meet over by that security desk in half an hour. Surely among the three of us we can find her."

Carole smiled. "That sounds like a good idea to me."

They split up. Stevie took the two large department stores at either end of the mall; Lisa took the smaller stores on one side of the mall, and Carole the stores on the other side. A half hour later they met near the security desk.

"Any luck?" said Carole, out of breath.

"No." Lisa shook her head. "Everybody I saw was either too young or too old. How about you?"

"I saw one woman the right age, but she had another little child with her. Unless Cynthia's got a mystery twin, it wasn't her."

Both girls turned to Stevie. "Well?"

"I saw one woman who thought I wanted to kidnap her child, another one thought I was trying to shoplift a toaster, and another woman almost banged me on the head with her big red purse because she thought I was

93

trying to steal it." Stevie sighed. "There are some pretty weird women with red purses running around this mall!"

Carole laughed at Stevie's efforts, but she was still concerned about the little girl. "I don't know what to do now," she said sadly.

For a moment all three girls just sat there, staring at the flashing red light above the security station. Then Stevie snapped her fingers. "I know!" she said.

"What?" said Lisa and Carole.

"One of us can go up to the security desk here and tell the guard that her name is Cynthia and she's lost her mother. The security guard will announce it over the public-address system!"

"Won't they ask for a last name?" said Lisa. "That's one thing we don't know about Cynthia."

"Say it's too hard to pronounce," Stevie replied. "Have them say, 'Would a woman carrying a large red pocketbook please report to the security station? Your daughter Cynthia is lost.' "

"Wait," said Carole. "Cynthia might already be here with her mother this afternoon. She said her mother might come back and pick her up early."

"Well, if her mother stashes her at the library, she could easily stash her in some toy store here." Stevie shrugged. "It's a possibility, anyway."

Lisa and Carole looked at each other, knowing that

this plan had Stevie's fingerprints all over it, which meant it could end in disaster. But neither of them could think of anything else to do, and they both wanted to help the little girl.

"Well, okay," said Carole. "Who's going to be Cynthia?"

"I vote for Lisa," Stevie said. "She's the most logical, and the woman who thought I was after the toaster may have already described me to security!"

"I don't know," Lisa said. "I've never done anything like this before."

"Don't worry," said Stevie. "Carole and I will be close by, and if anything goes wrong, we'll create a diversion."

"Yeah, I bet." Lisa rolled her eyes. She looked at Carole and sighed. "Well, okay. Here goes nothing."

Stevie and Carole watched as Lisa walked over to the security station. She talked to a lady in a blue uniform for a moment; then suddenly the bouncy mall music stopped and a voice blared over the speakers.

"Shoppers, could I have your attention, please? Would a woman carrying a red pocketbook please come to the central security station? Your daughter Cynthia is here waiting for you."

Stevie gave Carole a high five. "It worked!" she crowed. "Lisa's a genius!"

"Right," agreed Carole. "Now let's just see who comes to get little Cynthia."

The girls sat and watched. It seemed as if hundreds of shoppers passed by, but not one person with a red pocketbook stopped at the security station. Suddenly Stevie jumped up.

"What is it?" asked Carole.

"It's Mrs. Atwood," replied Stevie. "Dead ahead!"

"Lisa?" Already they could hear Mrs. Atwood's confused voice. "Why are you talking to the security guard? Has there been some kind of problem?"

"Uh, no, Mom," Lisa's face turned red. "I just got separated from you."

"Are you Cynthia's mother?" The guard looked down at Mrs. Atwood.

"Cynthia?" Mrs. Atwood frowned.

"Look!" Stevie shrieked. "There's Cynthia!" She and Carole ran over and hugged Lisa as if they hadn't seen her in years.

"Cynthia?" Mrs. Atwood repeated. "You mean Lisa? Stevie? What are you doing here? And what is going on?"

"Lisa?" said the security guard, now puzzled as well.

"Yes," said Stevie, still clinging to Lisa and ignoring Mrs. Atwood. "Cynthia Lisa. Everybody calls her Cynthia except her friends and her mother. We call her Lisa. Cynthia L. Atwood."

"But I thought you said your last name was unpronounceable." The guard frowned.

"It is, it is," said Stevie. "We just call her Atwood because it's easy to remember."

"Now, wait just a minute—" began the guard.

"Look!" cried Carole. "There's that blouse I've been dying to look at. Let's go grab it before someone else buys it! Come on, Mrs. Baghdahnoviztzchki . . . er, Atwood, you come, too!"

Stevie, Carole, and Lisa headed quickly over to the blouse. Mrs. Atwood shrugged at the security guard. "Thanks," she said, scratching her head. "I'm not sure what for, but thanks just the same."

"Not a problem," the guard said, looking at the three girls and shaking her head.

By the time Mrs. Atwood reached the blouse display, the girls had decided it wasn't the right color for Carole.

"Anybody want to shop for anything else while we're here?" asked Mrs. Atwood, still puzzled over the scene with the security guard.

"Not me," said Carole.

"Me either," said Stevie. "I'm really broke now."

"Well, then let's just go home," said Mrs. Atwood. "Stevie, I'll give you a ride if you'd like. I have to say, girls, this is the strangest shopping trip I've ever made."

They trooped back to Mrs. Atwood's car. The three girls sat in the back, dying to talk about little Cynthia but not daring to in front of Mrs. Atwood. Finally Stevie broke the awkward silence.

"I'm really glad we bought that dog for Veronica," she said. "But I think I'll wait until the day of the demonstration to give it to her."

"How come?" said Lisa. "I mean, why not sooner?"

"I don't know," replied Stevie. "It seems like Robespierre will either have recovered or not by then. If he's better, then the little china dog will be like a celebration. If he's not, well, then at least it will be something to remember him by."

"That's a good idea," said Carole.

"Yes, it is," Lisa agreed. "She'll really appreciate it then, one way or the other."

Carole frowned. "In the meantime, though, Stevie, if she's so upset about her dog, how are you going to manage the driving demonstration with her?"

"Oh, it won't be a problem," Stevie said confidently. "She's really pretty cooperative once you get past that hard armor she seems to always wear."

"Veronica?" Lisa said. "Cooperative?"

Stevie nodded. "We had a super-long talk the other day. I think we finally found common ground."

She settled back in the seat and smiled while Carole and Lisa looked at each other, both of them raising their eyebrows in doubt. They'd never known Veronica to work on common ground with anyone.

9

WEDNESDAY AFTERNOON WAS cold and cloudy, so riding class was held in the indoor ring. Stevie sat on Belle expectantly, watching for Veronica to lead Danny in. When Max began the class without her, Stevie knew Robespierre's condition must be grim.

"What's the matter with you?" Lisa asked as they warmed the horses up in an extended trot. "You look like you've lost your last friend."

"I was just thinking about Veronica," Stevie replied sadly. "She's not here today. I bet she's at poor Robespierre's bedside, just waiting for the end to come!"

"Oh, Stevie, you don't know that. Why not try to be optimistic?" Lisa said, smiling hopefully. "Maybe the dog got better and Veronica went shopping to cele-brate."

"Well, I guess that's a possibility," Stevie admitted.

"Anyway, you'd better pay attention in class now and worry about Veronica and her dog later, when Max isn't watching."

"You're right," said Stevie, trying to smile. "There's nothing I can do about Robespierre, anyway."

Riding class passed quickly, ending with one of Stevie's favorite exercises, in which the riders dropped their reins and jumped a series of cavalletti with no hands. Max congratulated the class on doing a good job, and soon all the riders except Stevie had brushed their horses down and were on their way home.

"Hey, Stevie, what are you doing this afternoon?" Carole asked as she and Lisa stopped by Belle's stall, their school backpacks slung over their shoulders.

"I'm going to work with Danny and Belle in the driv-ing harness," replied Stevie, holding up one set of the harness she'd cleaned over the weekend. "Red said he would help me."

"I would help you, too, except I've got to go to the dentist." Carole looked over at Lisa. "Could you stay and help Stevie this afternoon?"

Lisa shook her head. "I'd like to, but I've got this huge report in French due tomorrow, and I've barely cracked the book." She shrugged. "Sorry."

"It's okay," Stevie said with a smile. "I'll be fine. And Red will be terrific."

"Will you call us and let us know how it goes?" asked Carole.

"Sure," Stevie replied. "I'll talk to you both tonight."

Carole and Lisa left, and Stevie and Belle were alone. Stevie draped the heavy harness over her shoulder and clipped a lead line on Belle. "Come on, girl," she said, unlatching the stall door. "Let's go see if we have better luck learning to drive with Red than we did with poor Veronica."

By the time Stevie got back to the indoor ring, Red had the rest of the harness laid out. "Hi, Stevie," he called. "Are you sure you want to get into this now? It's pretty late in the afternoon."

"I have to, Red. Time's running out, and Veronica just can't be bothered with this right now."

"No kidding." Red's voice was tinged with sarcasm. "And when can Veronica be bothered with anything?"

"I don't know," replied Stevie. "But not now. She's got some problems at home."

"Yeah, right." Red gave a disbelieving snort. "How far did you two get the other day?"

"Not too far," Stevie admitted, remembering all the kicking and biting between Belle and Danny. "As equestriennes, it wasn't our finest hour."

"Then let's start from scratch and get these horses

101

accustomed to the harness. We'll fit Belle first, since you're used to working with her; then we'll fit Danny. I'll show you how all these little pieces of leather work together."

Stevie grinned. "Thanks, Red."

Explaining as he went along, Red began to show Stevie how driving tack was different from riding tack. There was a breech strap that stopped the wagon when the horse stopped, a crupper that kept the back pad from shifting forward on the horse's withers, and a checkrein that kept the horse's head in the right position. Though the bridles were similar, driving bridles came with blinders to keep the horse from seeing anything from behind.

"Why wouldn't they want the horse to see behind him?" Stevie asked as she carefully fit the blinders close to Belle's eyes. "It doesn't seem fair."

"Because if a horse doesn't know what he's pulling, he's okay with it," explained Red. "But if he looked back and saw a weird-looking thing like a wagon or a buggy right up against his tail, he might get scared and bolt or buck. Then you'd have a real mess on your hands."

"I never thought of that before," said Stevie, giving Belle a pat on the neck. "But I guess it's for their own good."

"Yours, too," Red said.

They worked a few more minutes on Belle, getting

the tack adjusted comfortably under her tail and around her shoulders. Then it was Danny's turn. Red brought him out slowly. Stevie wondered what he would do when he saw Belle in such a funny-looking harness, but he stood quietly when Red led him to the center of the ring and Stevie began to put the same contraption on him.

"Okay," Red said when Danny stood outfitted just like Belle. "Let's walk them around for a little bit and let them just get used to the way this stuff feels. You take Belle, and I'll take Danny."

"Okay," said Stevie. They walked the horses around the ring several times. Mostly the horses behaved as if they wore driving tack every day of their lives, although Belle twitched her tail against the crupper.

"I don't think they mind this too much at all," Stevie said, amazed.

"They're both doing well," said Red. "Let's attach the reins and you can drive them around the ring."

He clipped a set of reins to each bridle, then pulled the horses up side by side. "Okay," he said to Stevie. "Here are your reins. The two in your right hand are Danny's, the two in your left are Belle's. See if you can drive them around the ring." He frowned at her hands. "You brought gloves, didn't you?"

Stevie shook her head. "I didn't know I needed them."

"Try to remember them next time, or you'll get blisters."

"Okay." She took the reins and stepped back from the horses. With butterflies fluttering in her stomach, she looked over at Red. "What do I do now?"

He laughed. "Just say giddyap and see what happens."

"Okay," she said, taking a deep breath. "Here we go. Giddyap!" She popped the reins gently over both horses' backs, and all at once they began to move forward. Danny tried to push ahead of Belle several times, but mostly they walked side by side, with Stevie walking behind them. When they reached the end of the ring, Stevie didn't know what to do.

"How do I turn them?" she called frantically to Red.

"Just pull back on Danny a little. They should get the idea."

Stevie pulled back on Danny, but she pulled too hard. The big gray made a complete turn. Suddenly he was walking toward Stevie while Belle was walking away from her!

"Uh-oh," laughed Red. "You've got them going north and south at the same time! Stop them and let's try it again."

Stevie pulled Belle to a stop and managed to turn Danny around. They tried again. This time Belle wanted to charge ahead of Danny, and they seemed to bound around the ring in spurts, rather than with a smooth gait. The next time, both horses turned completely around when Stevie tried to negotiate the turn. After an hour of stop-and-go driving practice, Stevie, Danny, and Belle all stood before Red, sweating and exhausted.

"Wow," breathed Stevie with a wide grin. "This is hard work, but it's lots of fun!"

"You did okay," said Red. "Next time we'll see how they'll do hitched to the wagon."

"When can we try that?" Stevie asked excitedly. "We've only got about ten days before the demonstration for Cross County."

"How about Friday afternoon?" suggested Red. "Not much is going on here then."

"Great," said Stevie. "I'll be here right after school. And thanks, Red. You've been wonderful!"

"My pleasure," said Red with a grin. "Only next time, don't forget those gloves!"

Stevie untacked both horses and cooled them down, then put them back in their stalls with an extra forkful of hay. She was so excited about her driving success that she practically ran all the way home. She couldn't wait to tell Carole and Lisa how much fun driving was, but first she wanted to call Veronica and find out how poor Robespierre was doing. Maybe if the news was not good, hearing about how wonderfully Danny had done would make her feel better. As soon as she reached her house, she hurried upstairs to her room and dialed Veronica's number.

The phone rang once, then twice, then three times, and then an answering machine switched on. *"This is the diAngelo residence,"* a snooty voice said. *"Leave your message at the tone, and your call will be returned."*

Stevie frowned and hung up. She didn't feel comfortable leaving a personal message about poor Robespierre with the cold voice on the diAngelos' answering machine.

"Maybe I'll e-mail her," Stevie said aloud. "That way she can read my message and nobody else can hear it."

She looked up Veronica's e-mail address and hurried down to her father's study, where the Lakes kept their home computer. Fortunately none of her brothers was online or playing one of their space invader games, so Stevie had the machine to herself. She logged on, then began to type her message.

Dear Veronica,

  I just wanted to let you know how much I missed you in riding class today and how much I've been thinking about Robespierre. I hope he's getting better, but even if he's not, it helps to remember that things always work out for the best. I had a good workout today with Danny and Belle (Red O'Malley helped me). I made a bunch of mistakes, but the horses did great and learned a lot. I don't think you've missed too much. Red and I will be working again on Friday afternoon. It would be wonderful if you could join us, but if you can't, that's okay, too. Just remember that we're all thinking about you, and if you need me to do anything else for you, all you have to do is call.

Your friend,
Stevie

Stevie reread her message, then clicked on Send Now. She turned off the computer and smiled. Veronica would probably feel a whole lot better once she read that message. At least she would know that somebody who understood how people could feel about animals was thinking about her and cared about what happened to poor Robespierre.

10

"BYE, MOM!" STEVIE called as she walked out the door. "Thanks for lunch. I'll see you later!"

She heard her mother's muffled okay from the laundry room, then took a bite of her slice of still-warm gingerbread. There was nothing she liked better than finishing her lunch while she walked to Pine Hollow. She figured the eating part probably saved her five minutes of just sitting at the table, and the walking part gave her time to ponder what was going on in her life.

She sighed as she thought about what was going on in her life right then. Earlier that day she'd attended the Horse Wise meeting at Pine Hollow and taken her regular riding lesson. Veronica hadn't attended either of them, nor had she practiced driving with Stevie on Friday afternoon. Stevie had seen Veronica after gym class at school on Friday, but she'd been with a group of her own friends and they hadn't had any time to talk. Though she'd answered Stevie's e-mail, her message had only read, "Thanks. Okay. See you."

Stevie took another bite of gingerbread and frowned. The more she thought about that e-mail, the more uncomfortable she felt—as if she had poured out her heart to Veronica and Veronica had said nothing in return. Maybe she'd been wrong to express so much sympathy about Robespierre. Maybe that had upset Veronica even more, reminding her of something awful that she didn't want to be reminded of. Maybe Stevie should have said nothing about the dog and only told her about how good Danny was at learning to drive.

Stevie kicked a pebble across the street. Maybe she shouldn't have e-mailed Veronica at all. She shook her head. Sometimes when she tried her hardest to do the right thing, she wound up doing exactly the opposite.

Suddenly a familiar car came into view—a white Mercedes with dark-tinted windows. It was the diAngelos' car! Stevie gulped down her mouthful of gingerbread and smiled, but the car did not stop or slow down. It cruised past her, away from Pine Hollow.

"In the direction of Doc Tock's," Stevie said aloud,

turning and watching the car glide smoothly down the street and around a curve. Sudden tears stung her eyes as she imagined what must have happened. Veronica must have been at Pine Hollow waiting for her to come and work with the horses. Doc Tock had called to tell her that her dog was almost gone, and her parents had come to get her—to say a final good-bye to her beloved Robespierre.

"That's so sad," Stevie said, using her gingerbread napkin to wipe her eyes. She turned back toward the stable.

"Well, there's nothing I can do about Robespierre," she told herself. "That's all up to Doc Tock. But I can help Veronica by taking the driving-team pressure off her shoulders. That way she can concentrate on Robespierre's last days, and we can still have the best driving team Pine Hollow has ever had!"

Stevie finished her gingerbread and hurried into the stable. She walked directly to the locker room without even saying hello to Belle. There was something important that she had to do right away. In the back of her cubby, hidden behind a couple of old sweatshirts and wrapped inside a plastic shopping bag, was the elegantly wrapped package that contained the china dog she and Carole and Lisa had bought for Veronica. Stevie had planned to give it to her later, but now was the perfect time, when Veronica needed to know that someone was

110

thinking about her in her time of sadness. Surely Veronica would come to the stable soon, to be with Danny, the one remaining animal she loved.

Stevie sealed up the card she'd spent so much time choosing and wrote, "From your friends Stevie, Carole, and Lisa" on the envelope. Then she took the card and the package and put it in the top of Veronica's locker. *What a nice surprise that will be,* Stevie thought as the little present sat invitingly on the top shelf.

She closed the locker and hurried back out to Belle. She felt good about all the things she'd done to help her friend Veronica. Now the only other thing she could do was to get out there with Red and turn Danny and Belle into a real team of driving horses.

"I WONDER IF You-Know-Who is here today." Carole hurried up the library steps beside Lisa.

"Cynthia?" Lisa shrugged. "If she is, I don't think we can help her out too much today."

"I know," said Carole. "Our report's due in a week, and we really haven't gotten much done."

"We'll just have to work triple hard from here on out." Lisa held the big library door open.

Inside, the place was bustling with patrons. The girls looked for Mrs. Davidson and soon found her at her usual station, behind the checkout desk.

"Let's go get our forty-two books," whispered Lisa.

"Then we'll chain ourselves to a table until we finish."

"Right," Carole said with a grin.

They hurried over to Mrs. Davidson.

"Well, here come my helpers." She greeted them with a warm smile. "I've missed you girls."

"We've been busy at school this week," explained Lisa. "Are our books still on reserve?"

"They are until five o'clock tomorrow afternoon," Mrs. Davidson replied. "You want some help getting them to a table?"

"That would be great." Carole and Lisa both nodded. Mrs. Davidson helped them lug all the books to a library table. Then she had to go and help someone find an old copy of *The Washington Post*.

"Now," said Lisa in a stern voice as she pulled notepaper out of her backpack. "We've got to sit here and go through these books. We can't get up for anything! Not Cynthia or Mrs. Davidson or that little old lady who wanted us to look at her mushroom books! Nothing can make us leave these seats!"

"How about Veronica diAngelo?" Carole asked, blinking.

"What?" Lisa turned around in her chair. There, coming through the door, was Stevie's newfound friend, Veronica. As soon as she got inside, she stopped and sniffed, as if the library didn't smell good; then she waltzed over to the reserve desk. She looked at Lisa and Carole as she passed, but she acted as if she didn't recognize them.

"I don't believe it," whispered Carole. "Veronica diAngelo in the public library on a Saturday afternoon. Now I've seen everything!"

"Shhh!" said Lisa. "Be quiet and maybe we can hear what she's asking for."

The girls pretended to hunch over their books, all the while listening to what Veronica was saying to Mrs. Davidson.

"I assume you have some books on dogs," Veronica said in her snootiest voice.

"Yes, dear, we do," Mrs. Davidson replied sweetly.

"And where might I find them?"

"Have you ever been to a library before?" Mrs. Davidson asked.

"Of course I have," Veronica snapped.

"Well, you must know then that most libraries use the Dewey decimal system. Dogs are classified at 636.7. When you see those numbers on the spine of the book, you've found a volume on dogs." Mrs. Davidson smiled. "You might start over there, just past where those two girls are working at the table."

"Thank you," Veronica said archly. She turned and walked past Lisa and Carole, again barely giving them a glance.

After she passed, Lisa and Carole looked at each other.

"This must really be serious," Lisa whispered. "Veronica's actually asking the librarian where the dog books are."

"I know," Carole replied. "She must be doing research to help Doc Tock figure out what's wrong with Robespierre!"

"Poor Veronica," said Lisa. "She must feel awful. I wonder if there's any way we can help?"

Carole shook her head. "I think the best thing is to leave her alone. She didn't really look like she was in the mood for company."

"You're right," agreed Lisa. "Anyway, we've got enough stuff of our own to do."

The girls returned to the thick tomes that were open on their table. Lisa started reading about how horses may have pulled some of the huge rocks that the Egyptians used to build the pyramids, while Carole took notes on how teams of horses helped build the Erie Canal. Suddenly they heard a strange yet familiar noise. They both stopped writing and looked up.

"Did you hear that?" asked Carole.

Lisa nodded.

"Is it who I think it is?" Carole frowned.

"I don't know," said Lisa. "Let's listen harder."

114

They put their pencils down and concentrated. Ever so faintly, they heard two voices, arguing.

"Shhhh!" one voice said. "No!"

"Please?" another voice whined. "Pretty please?"

"What are you doing here, anyway?" replied the first voice.

"It won't take long," insisted the second voice.

"No, I will not!" the first voice snapped. "You need to go someplace else. You're in my way!"

Lisa and Carole looked at each other and got up from the table at the same time. Sometimes the library could be full of pesky people who just wouldn't leave other people alone. Veronica shouldn't have to deal with one of them today, particularly when she was doing research to try to save her dog!

"We'll just go and rescue her quickly," said Carole. "Then we'll leave her alone to deal with her problems in her own way."

"Right," Lisa said. "That's exactly what we'll do. It shouldn't take more than a minute."

The girls walked down the aisle together, then turned the corner. Their mouths fell open. It wasn't just another library pest who was bothering Veronica— it was Cynthia! She had parked herself in front of the dog books and was trying to get someone to read to her. She still had *Misty* clutched against her chest. All four girls turned and looked at each other, unbelieving.

"Cynthia?" said Carole.

"Lisa?" said Cynthia.

"Veronica?" said Lisa.

"Carole?" said Veronica.

"Cynthia!" yelled a voice so stern they all jumped. They turned. Mrs. Davidson was standing there, her pretty eyes flashing with anger. "Carole, Lisa, Veronica, will you excuse us, please?"

They had no choice but to leave immediately.

"OKAY, STEVIE. TRY it once more. Walk them down to the end of the ring, then make a wide turn and go into a trot." Red looked up at Stevie, who was perched in the Pine Hollow wagon, reins in hand.

"You think I can do it?" Stevie's face was flushed with excitement. All Sunday afternoon they'd been working with the horses hitched to the wagon. It felt funny to drive two horses from a seat high above them, but Danny and Belle had responded to her aids better than she had ever dreamed.

"Give it a go and see what happens," urged Red.

Stevie settled herself on the seat and flicked the reins over the horses' backs. At the exact same moment, they began to pull together, Danny on the left, Belle on the right. Stevie let the reins rest lightly in both hands as the horses walked down the ring, then pulled Danny ever so gently to the left. He made the inside turn, with Belle following on the outside. So far, so good. Then she had to ask for a trot. She took a deep breath, then tightened her fingers on the reins and flicked the long whip over their heads. After a moment's pause, both horses reached forward in an extended trot, the wagon rumbling loudly behind them.

"Look!" Stevie cried to Red. "We're trotting!"

"You sure are," he said proudly. He watched as they trotted once around the ring. Stevie turned them and pulled them to a halt in the middle.

"Wow!" Stevie said. "Wasn't that great? Aren't they terrific horses?"

"You bet they are," agreed Red, giving Danny a well-deserved pat on the withers. "But why are you holding your hands so funny?"

Stevie looked down. She was holding her fingers wide apart. "I keep forgetting my gloves," she admitted sheepishly. "My hands are a little sore."

Red grabbed her left hand and looked at it. Each finger had a bright red blister where the reins had rubbed it raw. "Does your right hand look as bad as this?" he asked with alarm, his eyes full of concern.

"Well, kind of," Stevie said, wishing she hadn't left her gloves at home.

"Then get down off that wagon, Stevie. You're done for the day."

"But I can't be done for the day, Red," she pleaded with him. "Our demonstration is only six days away. I've got to do better than my very best if I'm going to do both mine and Veronica's part and still impress Phil."

Red snorted. "Is that what this is all about? Impressing Phil?"

"Well, kind of. But not really. I mean, I always want to impress Phil, but this time Veronica is the one who really needs my help."

"And tell me when Veronica doesn't need someone's help." Red crossed his arms over his chest.

Stevie frowned. "I know you have to do a lot of her work for her, but this time she's really in bad shape. Her little white poodle, Robespierre, is dying! Veronica can hardly talk about it, but she's constantly at Doc Tock's office with him, and she's even gone to the library to do research on dog diseases. She's desperate to find a cure."

Red's eyebrows lifted in surprise. "And you're coming to her rescue over this driving demonstration? I didn't think you guys were friends at all. In fact, I didn't think you could stand each other."

"Well, for a long time we couldn't, but we had a long talk in the back paddock, and she's really nice once you get to know her. She loves animals just as much as we all do, and she's heartbroken about her dog." Stevie's eyes brightened. "Carole and Lisa and I even pooled our money and bought her a little china dog from the BonTon gift shop, just to make her feel better about Robespierre. It's in her cubby right now. I can't wait for her to get back to the stable to see it!"

Again Red looked surprised. "Stevie, I don't know about any china dog, but Veronica has already been here today. She came by earlier to pick up her riding clothes. She was muttering something about having to get them dry-cleaned 'before the dumb demonstration Saturday.' "

"Really?" Stevie blinked. Surely Veronica had seen the gift on the top shelf of her cubby—it would have been impossible to overlook. She must have taken it home. Still, wouldn't she have called or e-mailed or something? Stevie shook her head. Veronica wouldn't be intentionally rude. Her concern over Robespierre must have crowded out every other thought in her head.

"Look," Red was saying. "Don't think about Veronica and any little china dog now. You need to take care of those hands immediately. Go wash them, then get the first-aid kit and rub some ointment into them, then put some gauze over the blisters. Since you shouldn't ever leave horses unattended when they're harnessed to a wagon, I'll wait here and help you unhitch everybody when you get fixed up."

"Okay," Stevie said. "If you're absolutely, positively sure we can't do any more work today."

Red looked at her hands and shook his head. "We're done for the day. And tomorrow, too."

Stevie reluctantly climbed off the wagon. As much as she wanted to work longer, she knew Red was right. Her hands needed to be in great shape for next weekend, and that meant taking care of them now. She hurried in and washed them, then applied the ointment and bandages that Red had suggested. She was on her way back to the indoor ring when she passed the locker room.

"Maybe I'll stop in and see if Veronica really did get her gift," she said softly to herself. "Maybe Red was mistaken."

She tiptoed into the empty locker room and headed straight for Veronica's cubby. Slowly she opened the door. Veronica's good riding clothes were gone, but stuffed carelessly back in the top shelf of the cubby was the package Stevie had been so proud of. The beautiful wrapping paper was crumpled up in a ball, and the pretty little china dog lay half out of the box. Veronica hadn't even bothered to open the card that Stevie had spent so much time selecting.

"Oh, no!" Stevie found it hard to believe what she

was seeing. "The china dog was a terrible mistake. It must have upset her even more than I could have possibly imagined!"

Quickly she closed the door of Veronica's cubby. This was awful. The gift that she and Carole and Lisa had spent so much money on had only made everything worse. How could she have been so insensitive?

She hurried back to the indoor ring. Once again she felt as if she had done exactly the wrong thing. Now all she could do to make things better for Veronica was give absolutely the best, most perfect riding demonstration that it was in her power to give.

"Does that feel better?" Red asked, looking at her bandaged hands.

Stevie nodded, having forgotten all about her blistered fingers. "Do you think they'll be okay for the demonstration Saturday?"

"They will if you take care of them," said Red, helping her unhitch first Danny, then Belle. "I've had lots of blisters, and the trick is to just go easy on them until they heal." He looked at her and smiled. "Anyway, even with bum hands, you're more than ready to give a demonstration."

"You really think so?" It was hard for Stevie to unbuckle all the tiny harness straps with her bandaged fingers, so Red did that while she held the horses.

"Well, you might not be up to competition driving yet, but I don't think this joint meeting of Horse Wise and Cross County will present any problems for you."

"And Veronica will be there to help me," Stevie said as Red unbuckled Danny's halter.

Red laughed. "Absolutely," he agreed. "Just as much as she always is."

Stevie sighed. She and Red clipped the lead ropes to Belle and Danny, then led them back to their stalls. She wished Red had as much confidence in Veronica as she did, but maybe he was one of those people who had to see things before they would believe them. Well, he'd be surprised when Veronica showed up Saturday, ready and willing to help.

"Thanks again for all your coaching, Red," Stevie said as she put Belle in her stall. "You've been super."

"I've enjoyed it, Stevie." He turned to her and grinned. "I think you could turn into a real whip."

"Huh?" Stevie frowned.

Red said, "That's what they call someone who drives a carriage."

"Thanks!"

Stevie gave Belle a farewell carrot, then hurried out into the frosty afternoon air. She had a lot to do when she got home. She was going to e-mail Veronica the minute she got there and tell her not to worry about the driving demonstration. "We are going to be ready for next Saturday," she said, composing her letter out loud. "We are going to be great." She flexed her sore hands and felt her blisters. "Oh," she added. "Don't forget your driving gloves!"

12

"WELL, THIS IS it," said Lisa as she and Carole hurried up the steps to the library. "It's Sunday afternoon and our last chance to do any research before next Saturday."

"I know," Carole said glumly. "I just wonder how much we can get done. There are still forty-two books in there that we've barely glanced at."

"Can I make a suggestion this time?" Lisa turned to Carole, her blue eyes serious.

"Sure." Carole replied.

"Let's see if Cynthia's there before we get started. Then we can tell her right up front that we won't be reading any more of *Misty* to her."

"Good idea," agreed Carole. "Can you believe she

was actually trying to get Veronica to read to her yesterday?"

Lisa giggled. "Poor kid must really be desperate!"

They hurried inside the main reading room and put their backpacks down at their regular table. "Let's get this over with now," said Lisa. "Then we can get to work."

Carole nodded. Together they walked quietly back to the corner where Cynthia usually hung out. There was nothing there but books and the little chair she'd always sat on.

Carole frowned. "That's weird. Where do you think she is?"

"I don't know," said Lisa. "But let's look around some more before we get involved in driving history."

They walked up and down the shadowy stacks, but Cynthia was nowhere to be found. Even the tiny desks in the children's section were empty.

"Do you think her mother kept her home today?" Lisa asked as they started to walk back over to their table. "Or maybe Mrs. Davidson threw her out of the library for good."

"She could have, I guess." Suddenly Carole stopped and pointed at another long study table. "Wait. Look over there. Isn't that a little blond five-year-old head bent over that book?"

Lisa nodded. "Sure looks like one to me."

The girls walked over to the table. Sure enough, Cynthia sat there, quietly looking at the pictures in *Misty*.

"Ahem." Carole cleared her throat sharply. Cynthia looked up with a start.

"Oh, hi, Carole. Hi, Lisa," she said, her voice barely above a squeak.

"Hi, Cynthia," replied Carole. "How come you're sitting out here in the open and not hiding in the stacks?"

Cynthia's face grew red. "My mom wants me to sit here so she can keep an eye on me."

"An eye on you?" Lisa frowned and sat down in the chair across from Cynthia. "How can she keep an eye on you if she's shopping at the mall?"

"Uh, she's not at the mall today," Cynthia explained quickly.

"Oh?" said Carole. "Is she here?"

Cynthia nodded.

"Where?"

Cynthia gave a big sigh. "Right over there," she said softly, pointing to the checkout desk.

Carole and Lisa turned and looked. Only Mrs. Davidson stood there, rummaging through a large red pocketbook that sat on the counter in front of her.

Both girls turned back to Cynthia. "You mean your mother is Mrs. Davidson?" Lisa cried.

Cynthia lowered her eyes and nodded again.

"So she wasn't abandoning you to go shopping at all." Carole quickly pieced together the parts of the puzzle. "She was right here the whole time."

"I didn't want to stay at home with a baby-sitter," Cynthia explained in a small voice. "My dad is out of town on a business trip."

"But why were you hiding from your own mother?" asked Lisa.

"Because I like to talk to people and kind of make up stories." Cynthia's cheeks were bright red now. "But what I really like is to get people to read to me."

"Yeah, just like we did," said Lisa.

"You guys were the best readers ever." Cynthia's eyes brightened. "*Misty* and you are my all-time favorites!"

"Cynthia, do you know how that makes us feel?" Carole frowned.

"Yes," Cynthia replied in a small voice. "You're mad, Lisa's mad, my mom's really mad. I can't hang out in the stacks anymore, ever!"

Lisa looked at the little girl. "But do you understand why we're mad?"

"Because you didn't really want to read to me?" asked Cynthia.

"No," Lisa explained. "Because you made us think your mother was mistreating you. We were very worried about you. We even tried to find your mother that afternoon we went to the mall."

"Yes," added Carole. "Lisa and I and another friend of ours made idiots of ourselves, charging up to women with big red purses on their shoulders. They thought we were crazy."

Cynthia cringed. She was clearly embarrassed at the trouble she had caused.

"The worst thing, though, is that you lied to us," explained Lisa. "That's a very bad thing to do. People don't believe people who don't tell the truth."

"Yeah," said Carole. "Now Lisa and I won't ever believe anything you say."

Cynthia looked down at her book. Big tears began to roll down her cheeks. "But I didn't mean anything bad." She sniffed. "I was just having fun." She looked up. "And you guys got to read *Misty* again!"

"Yes, but we needed to be doing other things!" Lisa cried. "We've got a report due next Saturday, and we haven't gotten anything done on it."

"What's your report about?" Cynthia asked.

"The history of driving horses," replied Carole. "We have to stand up and give a ten-minute presentation next Saturday at our Pony Club meeting."

"Just ten minutes?" asked Cynthia.

Lisa and Carole nodded.

"I don't think you have to worry," she said sweetly.

"What do you mean?" Carole asked.

"I mean, if you read all those books my mom got you,

129

you'd be talking for ten million minutes! You guys could give a ten-minute presentation on *anything* to do with horses, right now!"

Lisa and Carole looked at each other. "You know," Lisa said, "she may have a point."

"I know," agreed Carole. "Maybe what we need to do is just sit and organize what we already know."

Lisa smiled. "If we did that and added some pictures, then we'd be in good shape for Saturday."

"I've got lots of horse pictures at home," said Carole. "We could go over to my house, go through them, and pick the best ones that illustrate driving."

"So we're finished here?" Lisa asked.

"I think we are," said Carole with a grin.

"But—" cried Cynthia.

The older girls looked at her.

"We only have two more chapters of *Misty* left. Don't you want to find out what happens?"

"Only if you promise never to lie to get people to read to you again," said Carole.

"Never again," Cynthia said solemnly. "I promise."

"Okay, then." Carole pulled a chair up on one side of Cynthia while Lisa pulled one up on the other. "Let's see where we left off. . . ."

13

"Look," whispered Lisa. "The indoor ring is filling up fast. Everybody's here today!"

Stevie, Carole, and Lisa were looking through the doorway at the crowd of riders. All their friends from Horse Wise were there, and even more riders from Cross County were piling into the arena.

"There's Joey Dutton," said Stevie. "And Angela Ashbury, and look—there's Phil!"

"Why don't you go over and say hello?" Carole suggested. "We've got a few minutes before the meeting starts."

"Okay." Stevie started through the door, then turned back to her friends.

"How do I look?" She held out her arms. She was

131

wearing her best pair of breeches and a freshly washed and ironed white blouse. For once her blond hair was neatly combed, and her tall black boots gleamed.

"You look terrific." Lisa smiled. "Only tuck your shirttail in a little bit. It's coming out in the back."

"Thanks." Stevie pushed her shirttail back into the waistband of her breeches and hurried over to greet Phil. He was sitting in the front row, right beside his friend A.J.

"Hi, Stevie." Phil grinned. "It's great to see you!"

"Thanks." Stevie smiled back. "I'm so glad you guys got a good seat."

"What is it you're going to be doing?" teased A.J. "Driving some nags around the paddock?"

"Nags named Belle and Danny," Stevie said proudly. "Veronica diAngelo and I are giving a driving demonstration." Stevie looked up and searched the crowd for Veronica. So far, nobody had seen a trace of her.

"I'm really looking forward to this, Stevie," said Phil, glancing at the white gauze that was still taped to three of her fingers. "I know how hard you've worked."

"It's going to be wonderful," Stevie said, although she wondered how wonderful it was going to be if Veronica didn't show up. Well, if she had to do it all by herself, she would. She just couldn't look like a nitwit in front of Phil. He was really excited about this. She looked at him and smiled.

"I guess I'd better go get the horses hitched up. Will you meet me after everything's over?"

"I'll be right here." Phil patted a cooler beneath his chair. "I've brought lunch for everybody," he said with a grin.

"Great. See you later!"

"Hey, Stevie," Phil called as she began to hurry off. He gave her a thumbs-up. "Break a leg!"

"Right." Stevie laughed and hurried over to Belle's stall.

When she got there, Red was waiting.

"Any sign of Veronica?" he asked, raising one eyebrow.

"No." Stevie hated to admit that her partner wasn't there. "I guess she got held up."

"What a surprise," said Red. He looked down at Stevie's fingers. "How are your hands?"

"They're okay. Just three little blisters left."

"Did you remember your gloves?"

She nodded and pulled a pair of leather riding gloves from her pocket. "I don't leave home without them anymore."

"Good. Looks like I'd better help you get these horses hitched up, since your partner isn't here. You get Belle and I'll get Danny, and I'll meet you at the wagon."

Stevie thanked Red and gave Belle a quick scratch

behind the ears, then hurried to get the driving harness fastened on her. By the time she'd gotten all the straps tightened and the buckles buckled, the meeting was about to start. Quickly she led Belle out to the paddock, where Red already had Danny hitched to the wagon.

"Okay," he said, holding Danny still. "Back her in slowly, and I'll hitch her to the traces."

Stevie backed Belle into position, careful not to veer too close to Danny. When Belle was in the proper place, Red hitched the traces to the harness that went around her midsection. Stevie attached the long driving reins, adjusted the checkrein, and the Pine Hollow team was ready to go.

Stevie stepped back and admired the two expertly groomed horses standing in front of the shining Pine Hollow wagon. "Don't they look awesome?"

"They sure do," agreed Red. "Just like a real team of horses." He looked at Stevie. "You'd better go inside before Max starts the meeting. I'll stay out here with them until it's time for your demonstration."

"Thanks, Red," Stevie said as she hurried back to the indoor ring. "I don't know what I would have done without you!"

Inside, the stands were almost filled. Lisa and Carole were sitting near the front with Phil; Stevie had to search for a seat in the back row. Just as she was sitting down, she heard Betsy Cavanaugh give a little yell. "Look!" Betsy cried. "Here comes Veronica!"

Stevie turned. There, in the doorway, stood her partner. Stevie felt a warm wave of relief wash over her. Veronica had shown up! Stevie had known all along that Veronica wouldn't let anything stop her from fulfilling her responsibility. Red had been wrong about her. Veronica was every bit the teammate that Stevie had thought she was.

For the first time in two weeks, Stevie felt truly relaxed. All the extra work she'd put into this project had been worth it. Everything was going to be okay. She smiled as Max stepped to the center of the ring and began the meeting.

"Welcome, Cross County riders," he said. "We've got an interesting program for you today, all about driving horses as teams. We'll start out with some informative reports, then we'll end with a demonstration of two saddle horses pulling our Pine Hollow wagon. First, though, let's begin with the history of driving." Max smiled. "Lisa Atwood and Carole Hanson are going to tell us all about that."

Everyone applauded while Lisa and Carole walked to the front of the ring. Carole showed several posters that illustrated the various ways horses had pulled wagons throughout history, while Lisa read from a stack of note cards. Though Stevie already knew a lot of the information, Carole and Lisa added several things that were new to her. She'd never realized that horses had been used by people for such a long time, she'd never heard that they might have even helped the Egyptians build the pyramids, and she'd never known that sulkies were the lightweight rigs that trotters pulled in races.

"Wow," Stevie whispered to herself as Carole and Lisa ended their report and received another round of applause. "They really do know a lot about driving."

Polly and Anna gave their report on driving tack. Next there were reports on wagons and driving costumes. Everything was interesting, and the riders from both Pony Clubs cheered the presentations. Again Stevie felt butterflies in her stomach as Max stood to move the meeting outside.

"Okay. We'll take a five-minute break now. If everyone will move to the fence around the back paddock, we'll have a demonstration by our own Pine Hollow driving team."

Everyone began talking and moving slowly toward the door. Stevie struggled through the crowd, trying to reach Veronica. She had to find out about Robespierre before they got outside with the wagon.

"Veronica!" she called over all the noise. "Veronica!"

"Yes?" Veronica turned. Her eyes were bright and her cheeks were rosy. Her face showed no sign of tears or sorrow. Suddenly Stevie decided that maybe it would be better not to mention the dog right then. Why bring up a painful subject right before the demonstration? It might totally wreck Veronica's concentration.

"I just, uh, wanted to say hi," Stevie said. She leaned forward to give Veronica a supportive hug, but Veronica shrank back, horrified.

"Please don't do that!" she cried. "You might wrinkle my outfit!"

Stevie stopped and blinked. She hadn't noticed Veronica's outfit until then. It was like nothing she'd ever seen before. Veronica wore a pale gold riding coat that flared out from the waist. Ruffles covered the front of her creamy silk blouse, and she wore a shiny top hat with a lacy black veil that cascaded down the back. With her tall black boots, Veronica looked as if she were going to a costume ball instead of a ride in the Pine Hollow wagon.

"Did you remember to bring gloves?" was the only thing Stevie could think of to say.

"Of course." Veronica held up a pair of elegant black kid gloves. "They're made especially to match my boots."

"Well," Stevie said, suddenly feeling horribly under-

137

dressed in her simple boots and breeches. "I guess we're ready to go, then."

They hurried out to the paddock, where the riders were already gathered around the fence. Red stood waiting for them, holding both horses by their bridles.

"I see the whole team made it," he said, glancing slyly at Stevie.

"I always keep my appointments," snapped Veronica. She put one foot on the wagon wheel and daintily climbed up on the seat. Stevie climbed in from the other side, hoping that her shirttail was staying tucked in. Suddenly the crowd grew quiet.

"Okay, everybody." Max stepped into the paddock. "I'm pleased to introduce Veronica diAngelo and Stevie Lake, the Pine Hollow driving team."

Everyone clapped. Veronica smiled and picked up the reins and whip. Stevie held her breath. Was Veronica actually going to try to drive the wagon? She hadn't had a moment's practice! But then Veronica did something that she'd practiced all her life. With a brief nod to the audience, she passed the reins and whip to Stevie, as if she couldn't be bothered with actually driving the horses around the paddock.

"Ready?" Red asked softly.

Stevie nodded. "Let's go."

He let go of the bridles while Stevie gathered the reins. With a gentle flick of the whip above the horses' heads, Danny and Belle began to move as a team, pull-ing the wagon smoothly along the fence line. They started off at a slow walk; then, as the horses got accus-tomed to the brisk wind and the crowd staring at them, Stevie urged them into a trot. Everyone clapped.

She drove them in a big figure eight around the ring, the horses stopping and starting on her command. Once again the crowd began to cheer as Max stepped forward.

"I think Stevie and Veronica deserve a big hand," he said proudly. "They are both riders who've never driven a team before. And until two weeks ago, neither of these horses had worked together or pulled a wagon. I think that's wonderful teamwork!" Max looked at the girls and grinned. "Stevie, why don't you and Veronica take a victory lap and celebrate your success?"

Stevie grinned at Max and pulled the horses around for a final lap. She had just turned the far corner when a familiar white Mercedes pulled up and parked beside the paddock fence.

"Oh, look!" Veronica cried, standing halfway up in the seat. She waved her hand wildly. "My parents are here!"

Stevie could barely steer the wagon for Veronica's waving. She turned to catch a glimpse of what was so exciting. In Mrs. diAngelo's arms was a wiggling ball of fluffy white fur.

Robespierre! Stevie thought, her heart soaring with joy. *All Veronica's work and worry paid off! Doc Tock saved him!*

With a grin spreading across her face, Stevie pulled the wagon up in the center of the ring. Veronica was already halfway out of the wagon. "Wait, Veronica," Stevie said breathlessly. "I just wanted to tell you how glad I am that Robespierre's been cured."

Veronica's smile faded. "Robespierre?" she replied distastefully, wrinkling her nose. "You mean that old poodle?" She gave a little laugh. "Yes, Robespierre's been cured. Permanently. Dr. Takamura gave him a shot and it was all over. He didn't feel a thing!" She looked over at her parents and grinned. "That's our new little Sugarlump. My parents just picked her up this morning. She's so cu-u-ute! And her pedigree is much better than that other old dog's."

With that, Veronica hopped off the wagon and ran to her new puppy.

For a long moment Stevie couldn't move. Though she heard people clapping for her and Max's voice congratulating her, all she could do was sit there and watch as Veronica cradled the new puppy in her arms and let it cover her face with kisses.

"I can't believe it," Stevie finally whispered, still holding on to the reins. "I just can't believe it."

As Max dismissed the meeting, Red hurried out to the middle of the paddock.

"Is everything okay?" he asked worriedly. "You've been sitting there like a statue for the last five minutes."

"Yes, I'm okay." Stevie shook her head as if she were trying to wake up from a bad dream. "Someone I thought had changed a lot turned out not to have changed at all."

Red shrugged. "That happens sometimes." He looked over at Veronica. "Particularly when you're dealing with the diAngelos." He looked up at Stevie and smiled. "Try to see it this way, though. Today you became a real whip. Veronica will never be anything but a piece of baggage."

Suddenly Stevie heard other voices.

"Stevie!" Carole and Lisa ran up to the wagon. "You did a wonderful job!"

"Yeah, Stevie," said Phil. "Anytime I have a wagon to drive, you'll be the first person I call. You were terrific!"

Stevie grinned down at her friends. All at once she was very glad to see them.

"Hey, are we just going to stand around here admiring Stevie and her team, or are we going to eat lunch?" Phil held up his cooler invitingly.

"Let's help Stevie unhitch Danny and Belle," said Carole. "The faster we work as a team, the faster we can eat!"

"Good idea," said Stevie, once again smiling. "Everybody hop in the back and I'll drive us over to the stable."

Everyone piled into the back of the wagon, and Stevie clucked the horses into a trot. *How lucky I am,* she thought. *I've got a real team behind me.*

14

"THIS IS A great-looking lunch, Phil." Carole eyed the big blue-checked tablecloth Phil had spread out in the hayloft. On it were several different kinds of sandwiches and chips, some apples and oranges, various cans of soda, and a pile of huge chocolate chip cookies. Down below, in the stable, people were still milling around, but upstairs Phil and Carole and Lisa and Stevie were having a cozy, private picnic of their own.

"Thanks," said Phil. "Although you probably should thank my mom. She did most of it."

"Then tell your mom thanks." Lisa laughed. "Everything looks delicious."

Everyone grabbed what they wanted to eat and settled down in the soft hay. The sounds of Belle munching her own lunch wafted up from the stall below.

"Sounds like Belle's hungry," said Carole, peering down through the cracks in the hayloft floor. "She's worked pretty hard these past two weeks."

"So has Belle's owner," added Lisa. She looked over at Stevie, who for once was only picking at her sandwich. "What's wrong, Stevie? Are you too exhausted to eat?"

"No, I'm not exhausted," Stevie said quietly. "I think I'm still stunned."

"Still stunned?" Phil frowned. "How come?"

"Because I actually thought Veronica had changed," Stevie replied. "I actually thought she and I had become friends."

Phil looked over at Lisa and Carole, puzzled.

"Stevie and Veronica had a long heart-to-heart talk about Veronica's dog. She told Stevie that her dog was really sick and about to die," explained Carole. "Veronica actually cried real tears."

Phil almost dropped his turkey sandwich. "Veronica diAngelo cried? Tears?"

"Yes," said Stevie. "We thought she was totally devastated about Robespierre, but today her parents showed up with a brand-new puppy. When I asked Veronica about it, she acted like she could barely remem-

144

ber Robespierre's name. She said Doc Tock had put him to sleep several days ago."

"Oh, no!" Tears came to Carole's eyes. "That's terrible."

"That is terrible, but what's also terrible is the amount of extra work I put into this driving demonstration just to take the pressure off Veronica, who was supposedly distraught over Robespierre." Stevie's face grew red with anger. She held up her bandaged fingers. "I worked my fingers to the bone!"

Lisa said, "And we bought her that expensive china dog."

"China dog?" Phil frowned.

"We ran into Stevie at the BonTon gift shop. She told us about Veronica and her sick dog, so we chipped in and bought her this really expensive poodle figurine," Carole explained.

"And not once did she say thanks," griped Stevie. "She never even opened her card!"

"Oh, Stevie, don't you realize that's the real Veronica?" Carole asked. "What you saw that afternoon in the paddock was some kind of weird seizure. Veronica allowed herself to be a real human being for about ten minutes. Then she got over it and returned to her nasty old self. You just happened to be there for the whole show."

145

"That's right," agreed Lisa. "Veronica may have a heart somewhere deep inside her, but I wouldn't ever count on her revealing it for any length of time."

"You *are* right," Stevie said, finally taking a bite of her ham sandwich. "I should have known better. I should have remembered that Veronica will always be Veronica."

"You mean a despicable human being?" asked Phil.

"On her good days," replied Stevie with a laugh. She took another bite of sandwich, then turned to Carole and Lisa.

"Say, I've been meaning to ask you: Whatever happened with Cynthia and her mother?"

"Who's Cynthia?" Phil frowned again. "I thought we were discussing Veronica."

"Cynthia's this little kid in the library who did as big a number on us as Veronica did on Stevie," Carole explained.

"She had us convinced that her mother was dropping her off at the library while she shopped at the mall," continued Lisa. "But in reality, her mother was the librarian!"

Phil shook his head. "I don't get it."

Carole swallowed a bite of apple. "She made people believe she was practically an orphan just so she could get them to read to her. She was even pestering Veronica about it one day."

"You're kidding!" Phil said.

"No, it's true," replied Lisa. "She finally told us the truth, though. She knew what she was doing was wrong. She's got her problems, all right, but at least she's got possibilities, which is something Veronica will never have."

Phil leaned back against a bale of hay and smiled. "It sure sounds like you guys have accomplished a lot in the past few weeks."

Stevie looked at Carole and Lisa and laughed. "You know, he's right. I managed to let Belle and Danny get in a big fight and almost knock down the paddock fence. You guys started off researching driving history and wound up reading Misty to a little kid who told big whoppers about her mother."

Carole grinned. "And then we accosted all those women with red pocketbooks in the mall and almost got Lisa in trouble with the security guard."

"And then we spent all our TD's money on a china dog for someone we thought was heartbroken, but who really doesn't have a heart at all!" added Lisa.

They looked at each other for a moment, then all began to laugh.

"You know, Max wanted to teach us about teamwork

with these projects," said Carole, "but I think I already know all I need to about that."

"Me too," Lisa said, giggling.

"Me three," Stevie said, smiling at her friends. "I'm sitting here right now with the best team anybody could ever be a part of!"

ABOUT THE AUTHOR

Bonnie Bryant is the author of more than a hundred books about horses, including The Saddle Club series, Saddle Club Super Editions, the Pony Tails series, and Pine Hollow, which follows the Saddle Club girls into their teens. She has also written novels and movie novelizations under her married name, B. B. Hiller.

Ms. Bryant began writing The Saddle Club in 1986. Although she had done some riding before that, she intensified her studies then and found herself learning right along with her characters Stevie, Carole, and Lisa. She claims that they are all much better riders than she is.

Ms. Bryant was born and raised in New York City. She still lives there, in Greenwich Village, with her two sons.